THE ADVENTURES OF

The Bailey School Kids®

FRANKENSTEIN DOESN'T PLANT PETUNIAS

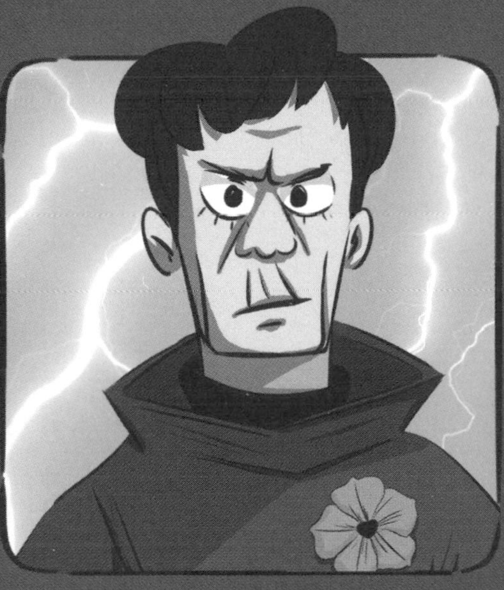

A GRAPHIC NOVEL BY PEARL LOW

BASED ON THE NOVEL BY

MARCIA THORNTON JONES & DEBBIE DADEY

graphix
An Imprint of
SCHOLASTIC

FOR KATELYNN ANDERSEN. MAY YOUR LIFE BE FILLED
WITH FLOWERS OF ALL SIZES! — MARCIA THORNTON JONES

FOR ALEX — DEBBIE DADEY

I DEDICATE THIS BOOK TO THE IMAGINATION WITHIN
ALL OF US; IMAGINATION THAT ALLOWS US TO SEE THE
WORLD WITH CURIOSITY, WONDER, AND AWE — PEARL LOW

Text copyright © 1993, 2022 by Marcia Thornton Jones and Debra S. Dadey
Art copyright © 2022 by Pearl Low

Library of Congress Control Number: 2021936601

ISBN 978-1-338-73663-2 (hardcover)
ISBN 978-1-338-73662-5 (paperback)

10 9 8 7 6 5 4 3 2   22 23 24 25 26

Printed in Mexico   189
First edition, August 2022

Edited by Jonah Newman
Book design by Steve Ponzo
Color assistance by Wes Dzioba
Creative Director: Phil Falco
Publisher: David Saylor

EDDIE

MELODY

HOWIE

LIZA

CAREY

MRS. JEEPERS

FRANK

DR. VICTOR

CHAPTER 1 FIELD TRIP

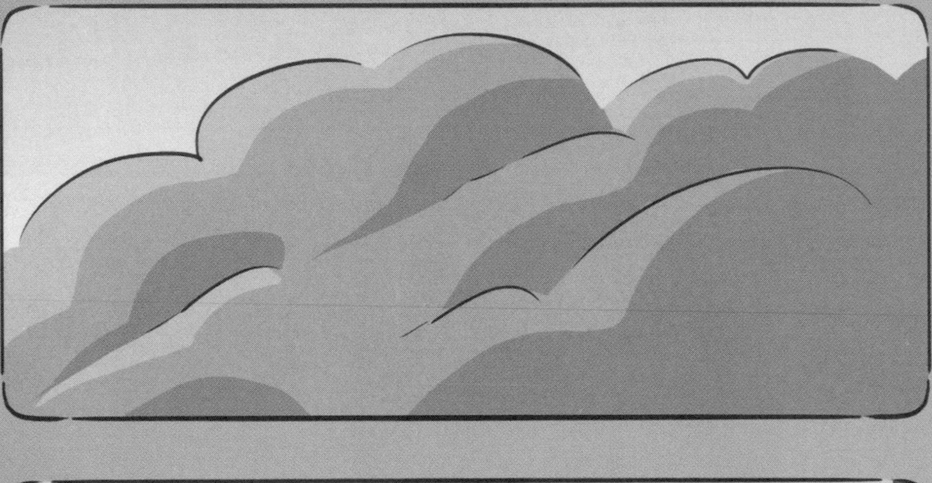

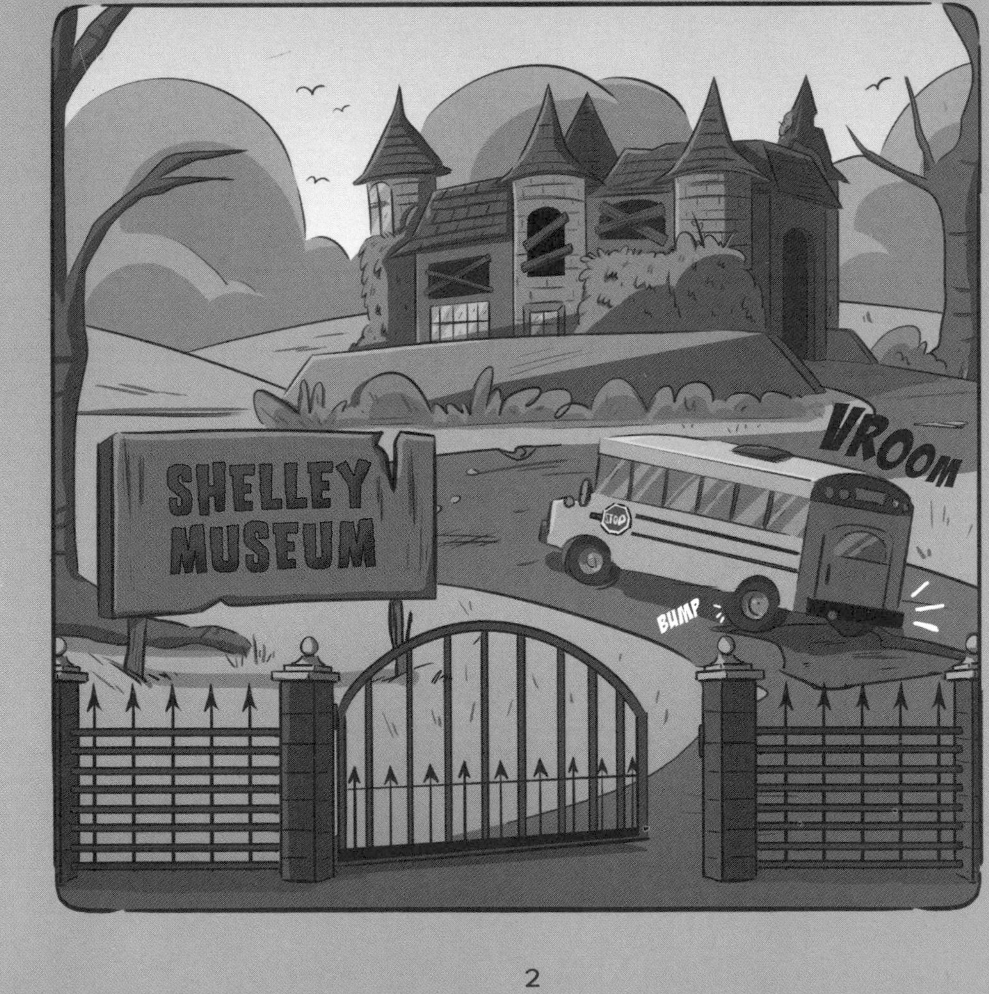
SHELLEY MUSEUM
VROOM
BUMP

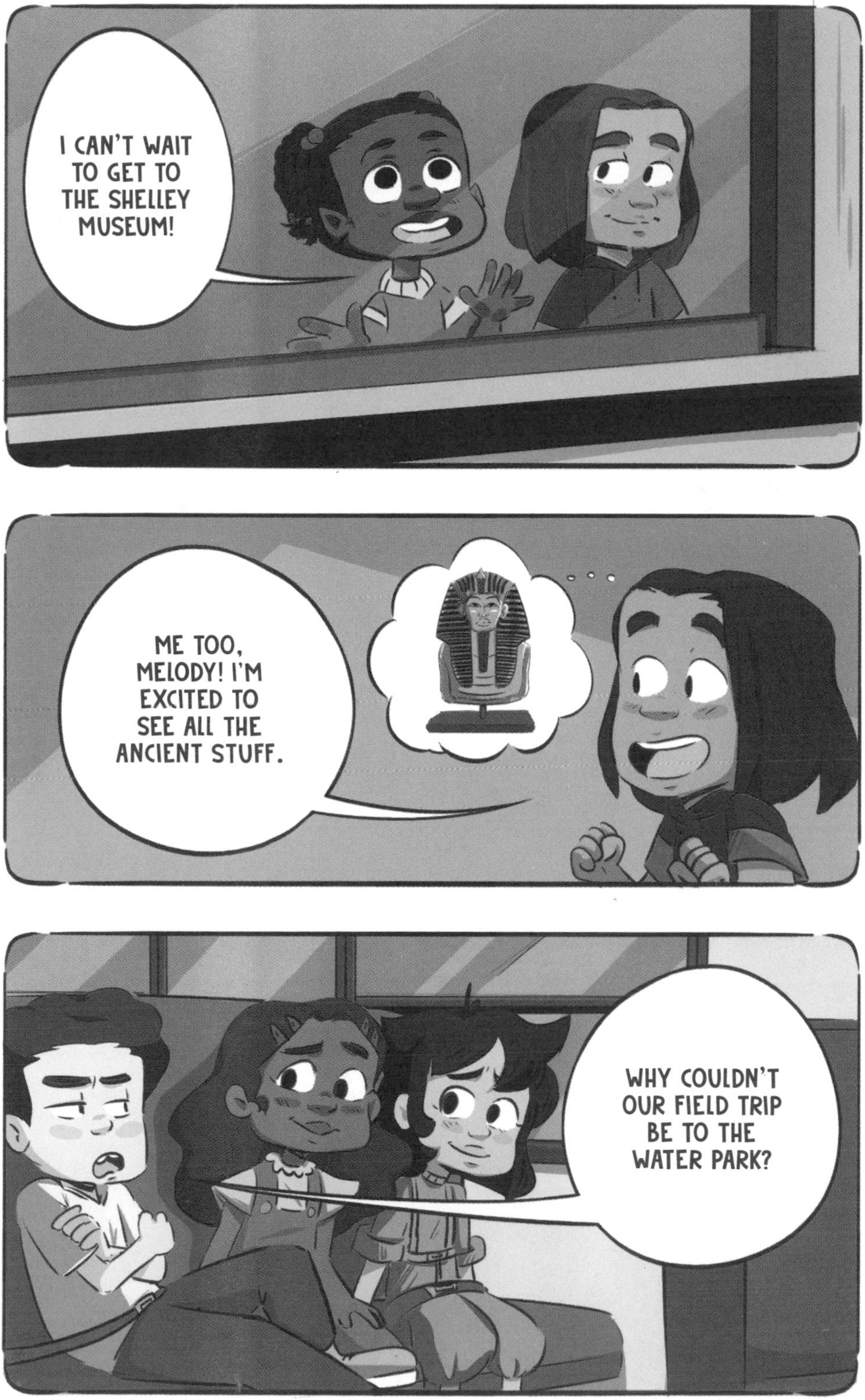
I CAN'T WAIT TO GET TO THE SHELLEY MUSEUM!
ME TOO, MELODY! I'M EXCITED TO SEE ALL THE ANCIENT STUFF.
WHY COULDN'T OUR FIELD TRIP BE TO THE WATER PARK?

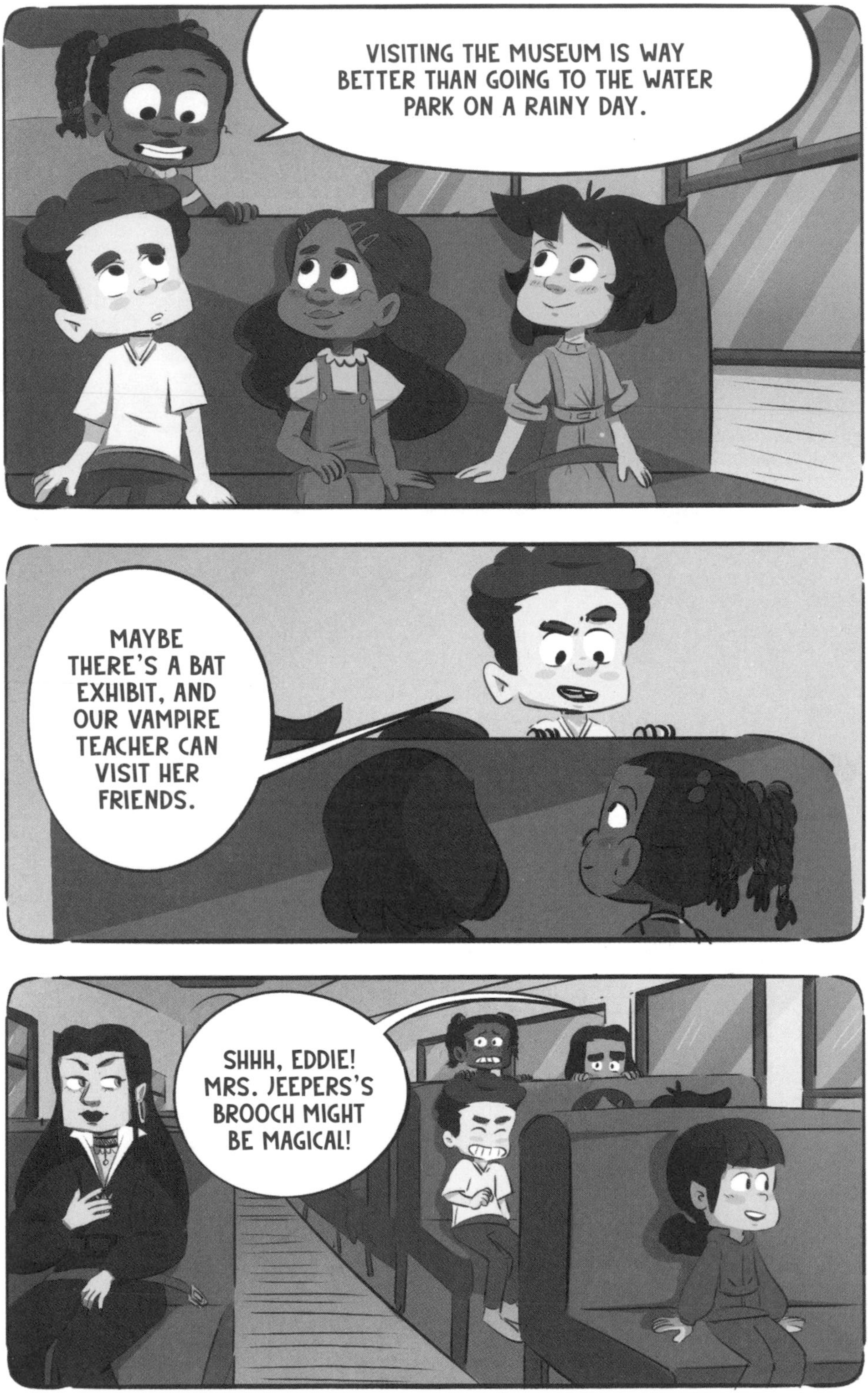
VISITING THE MUSEUM IS WAY BETTER THAN GOING TO THE WATER PARK ON A RAINY DAY.
MAYBE THERE'S A BAT EXHIBIT, AND OUR VAMPIRE TEACHER CAN VISIT HER FRIENDS.
SHHH, EDDIE! MRS. JEEPERS'S BROOCH MIGHT BE MAGICAL!

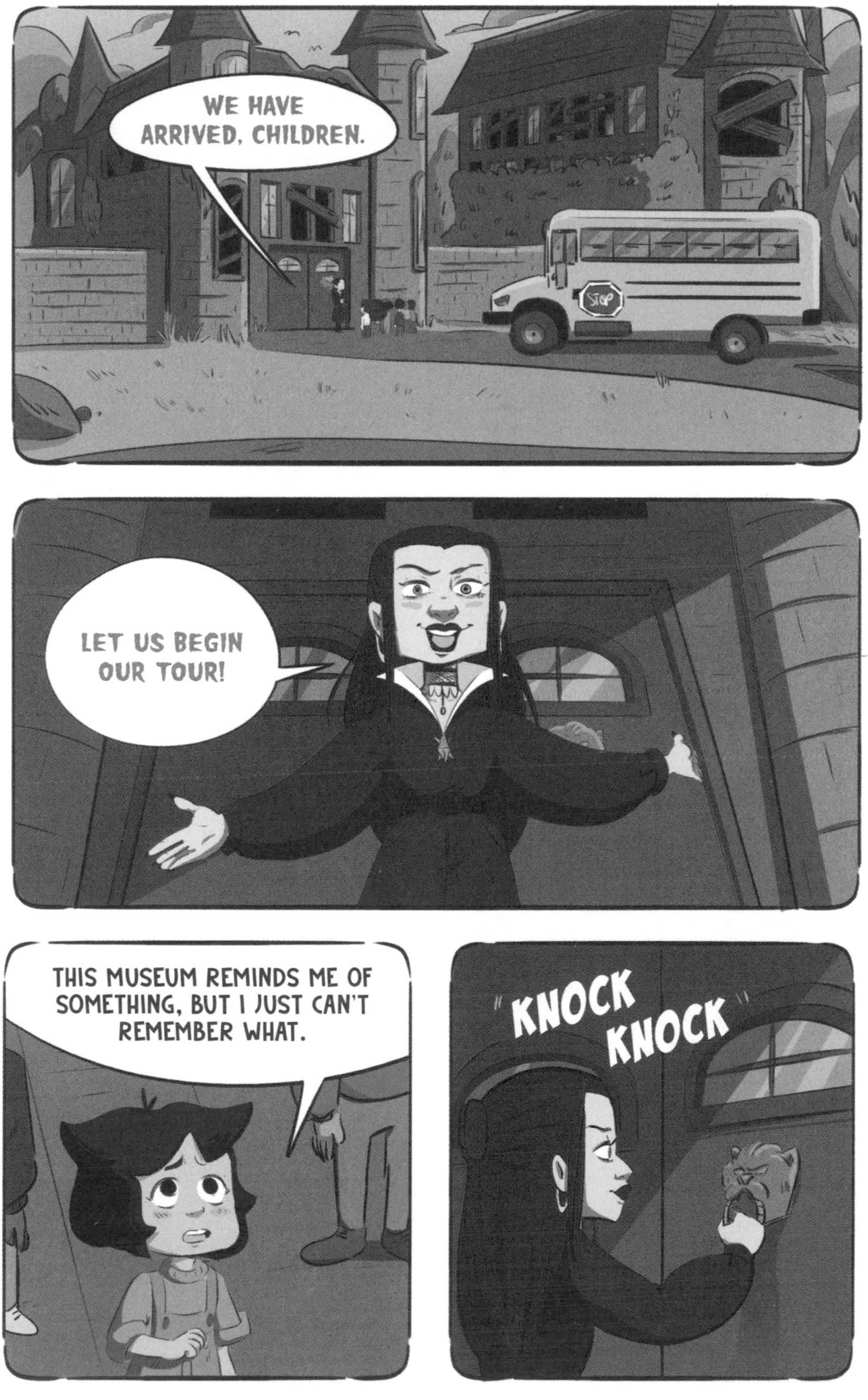
WE HAVE ARRIVED, CHILDREN.
STOP
LET US BEGIN OUR TOUR!
THIS MUSEUM REMINDS ME OF SOMETHING, BUT I JUST CAN'T REMEMBER WHAT.
KNOCK KNOCK

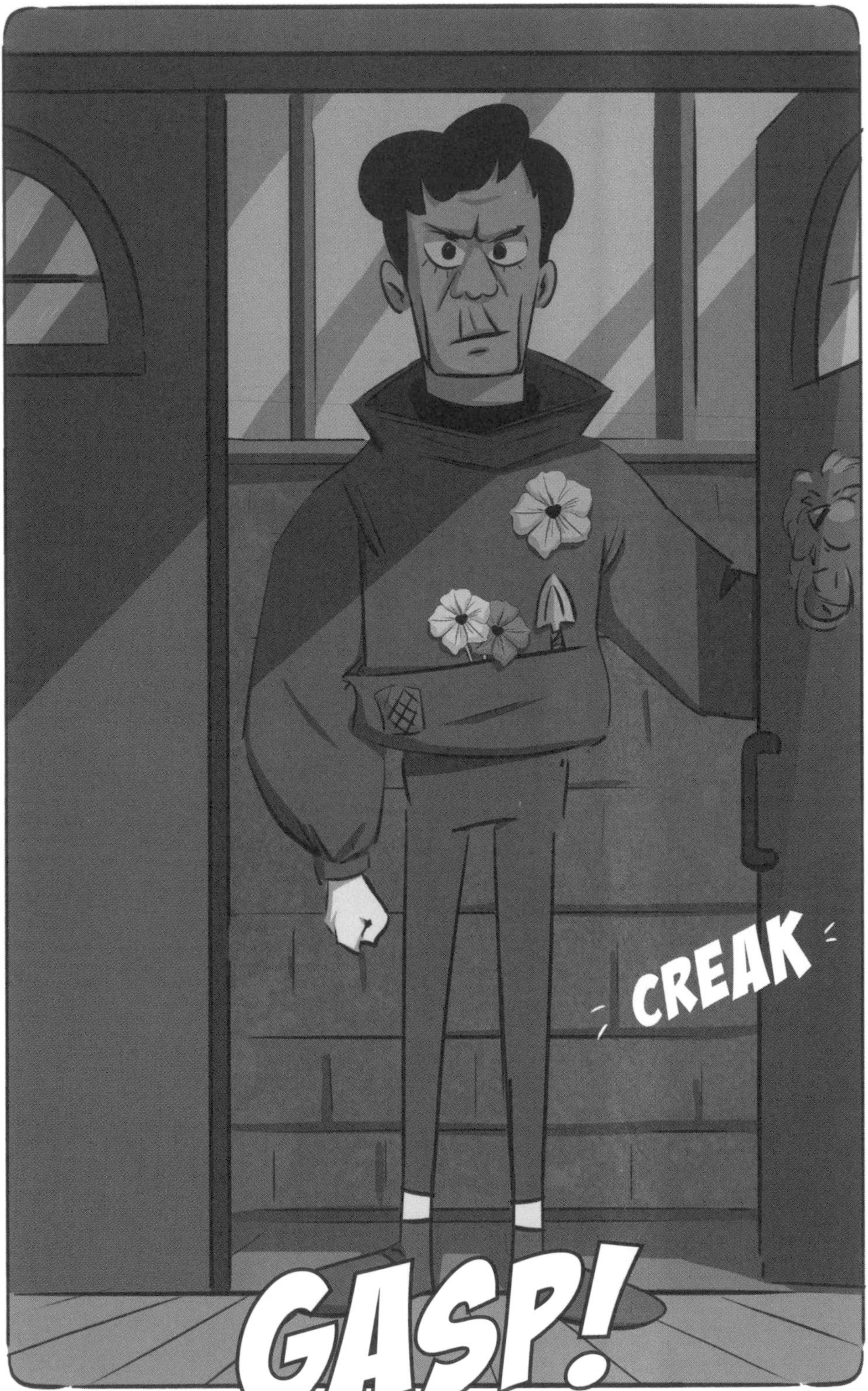
CREAK
GASP!

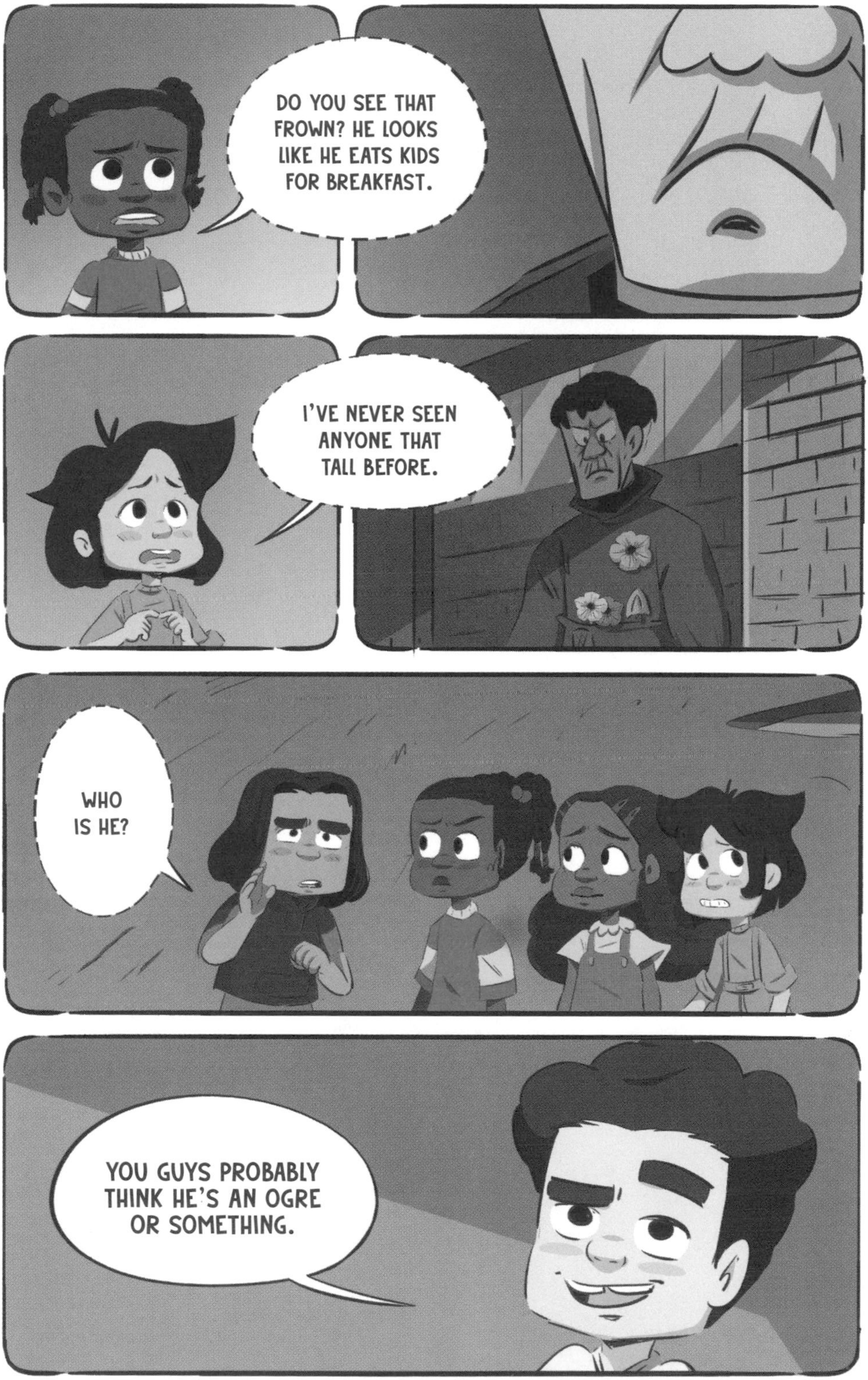
DO YOU SEE THAT FROWN? HE LOOKS LIKE HE EATS KIDS FOR BREAKFAST.
I'VE NEVER SEEN ANYONE THAT TALL BEFORE.
WHO IS HE?
YOU GUYS PROBABLY THINK HE'S AN OGRE OR SOMETHING.

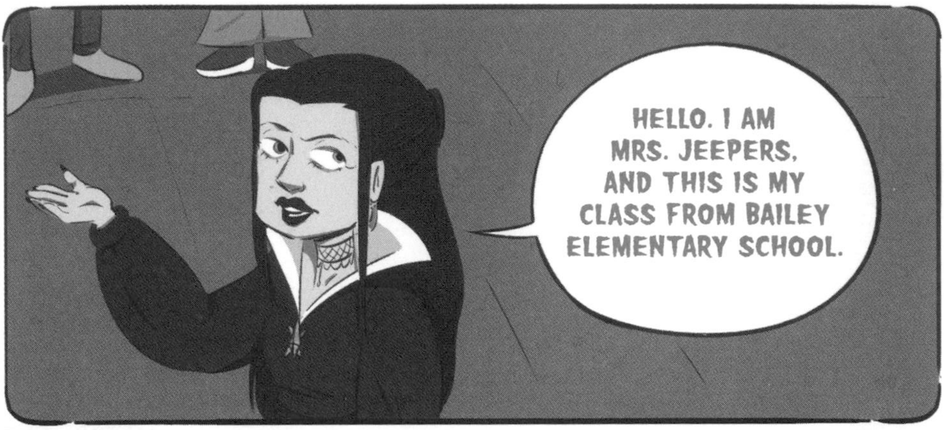
HELLO. I AM MRS. JEEPERS, AND THIS IS MY CLASS FROM BAILEY ELEMENTARY SCHOOL.

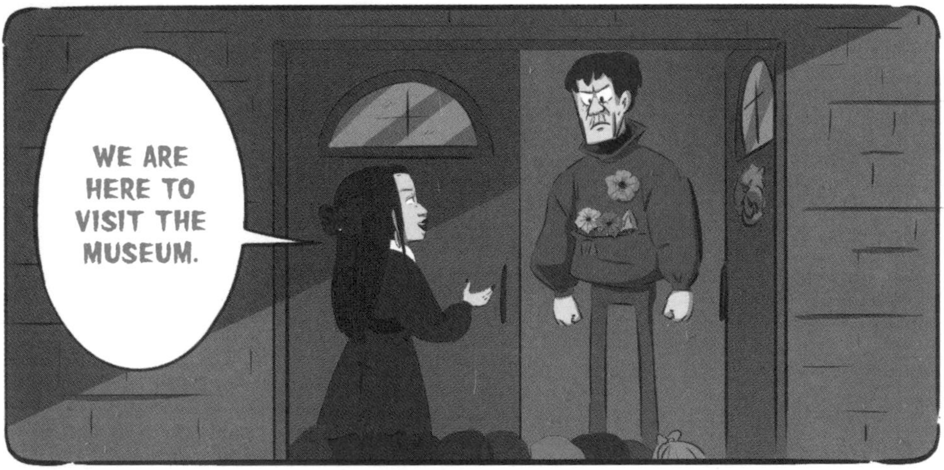
WE ARE HERE TO VISIT THE MUSEUM.

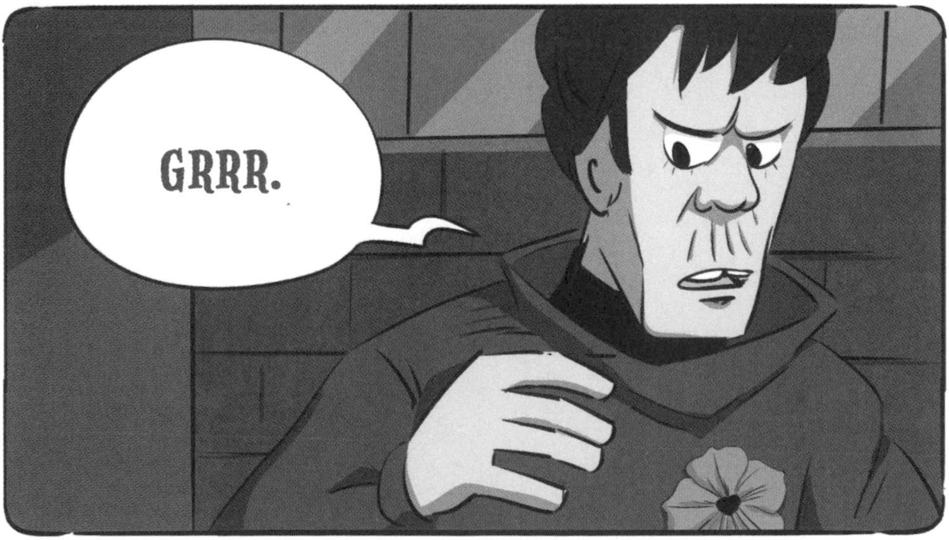
GRRR.

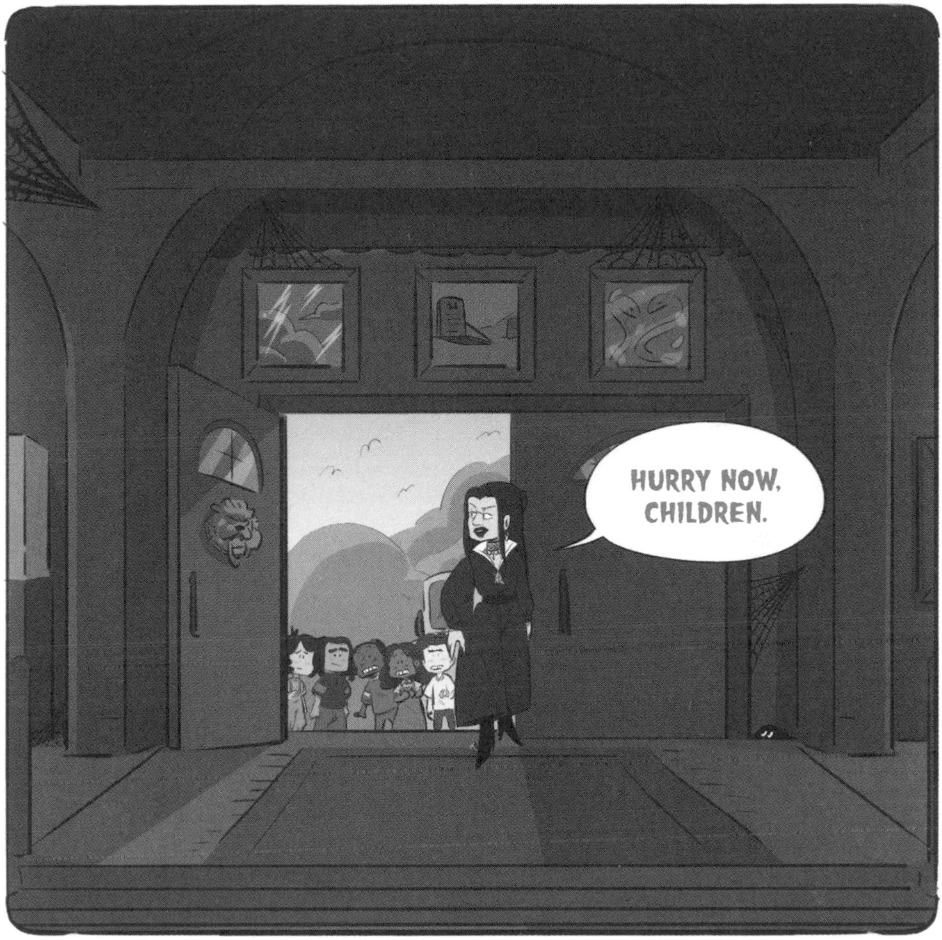
HURRY NOW, CHILDREN.

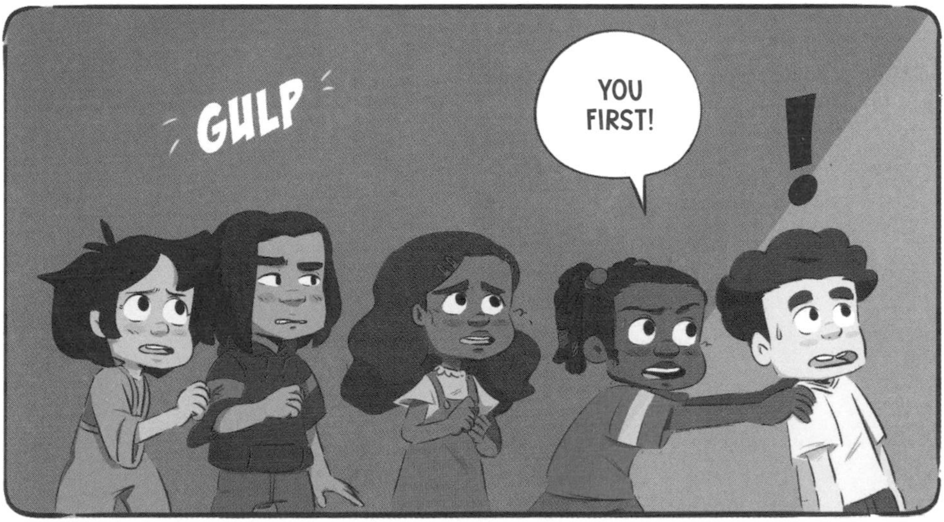
GULP
YOU FIRST!
!

CHAPTER 2 FRANKENSTEIN

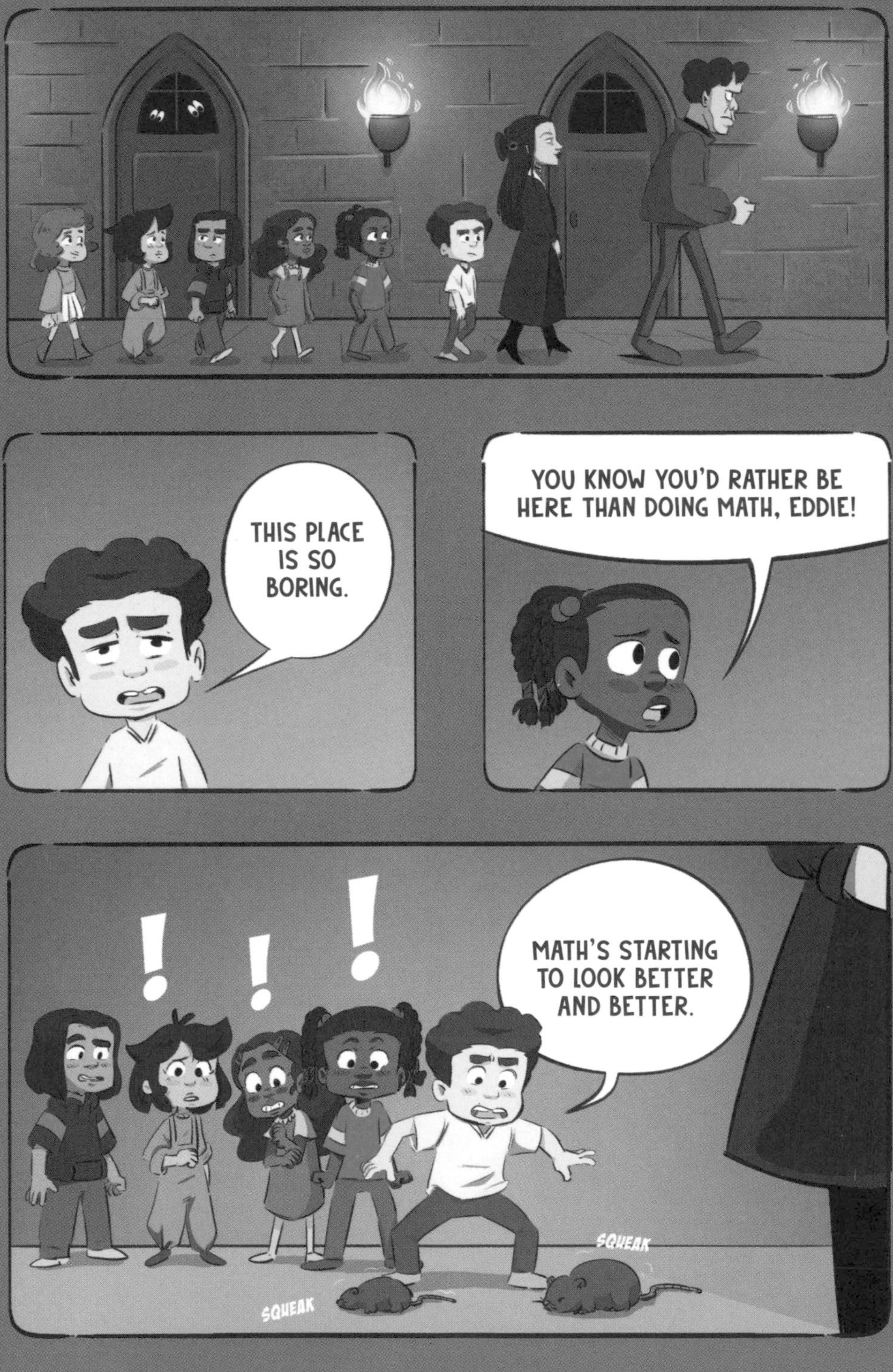

THIS PLACE IS SO BORING.
YOU KNOW YOU'D RATHER BE HERE THAN DOING MATH, EDDIE!
!
!
!
MATH'S STARTING TO LOOK BETTER AND BETTER.
SQUEAK
SQUEAK

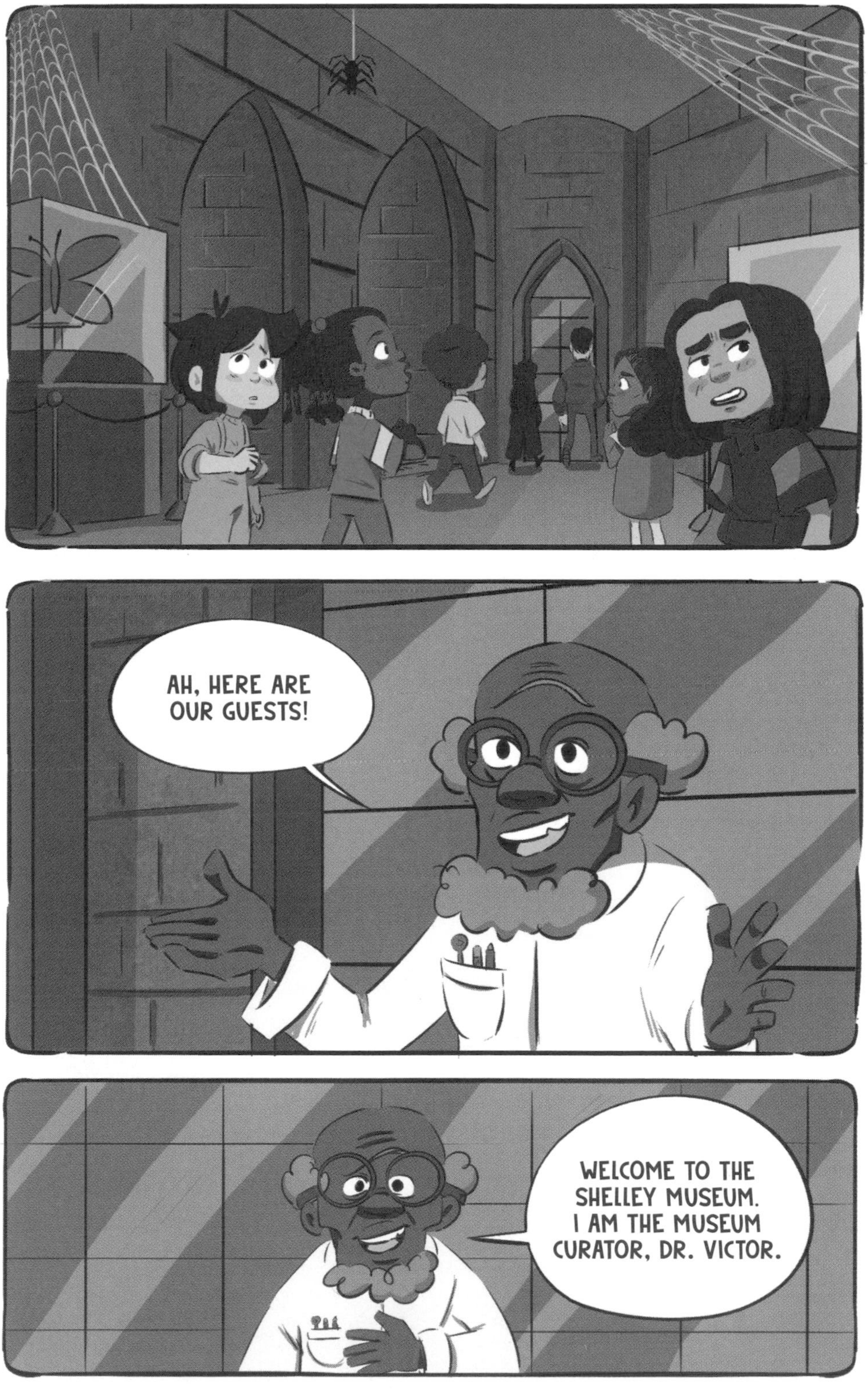
AH, HERE ARE OUR GUESTS!
WELCOME TO THE SHELLEY MUSEUM. I AM THE MUSEUM CURATOR, DR. VICTOR.

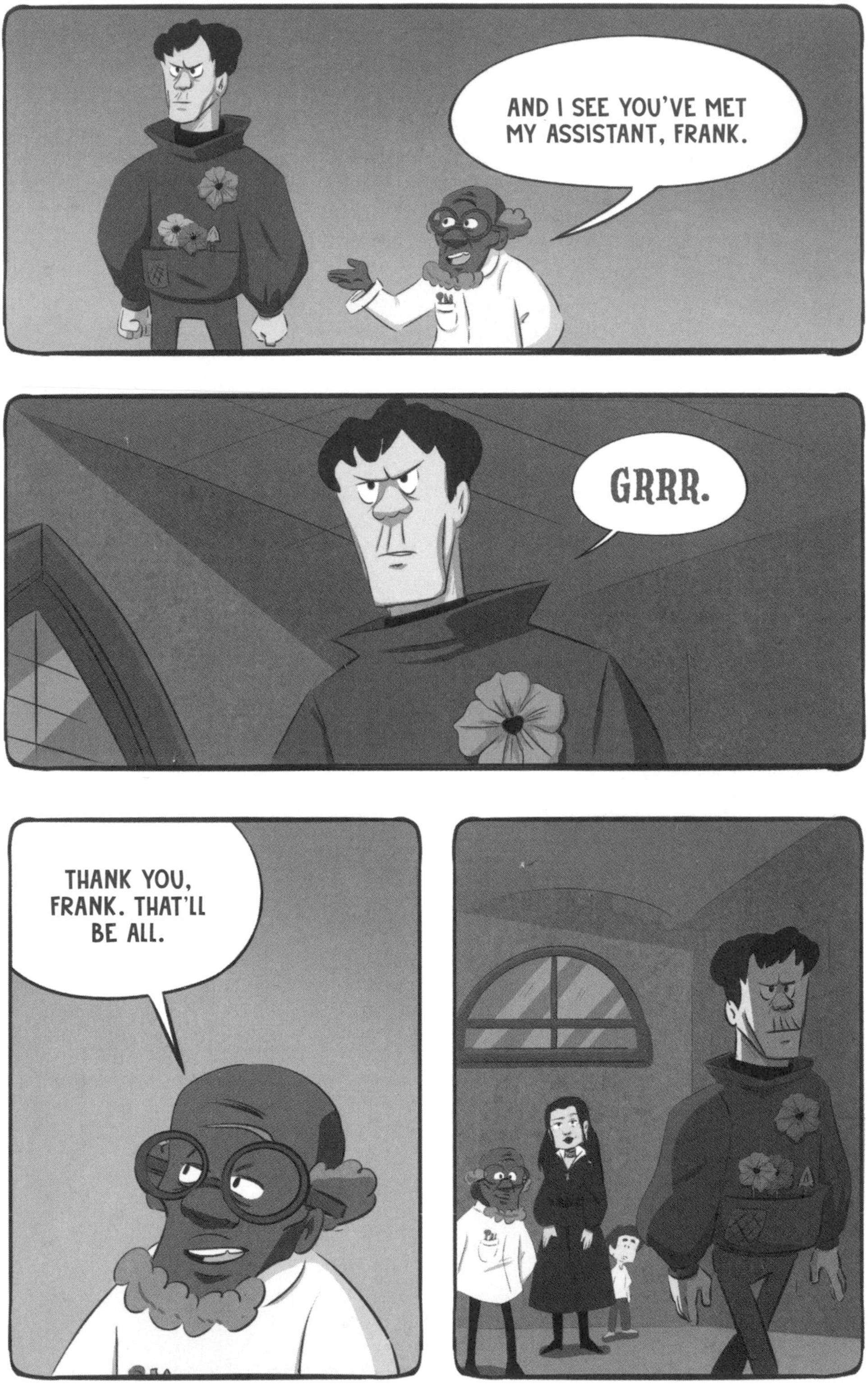
AND I SEE YOU'VE MET MY ASSISTANT, FRANK.
GRRR.
THANK YOU, FRANK. THAT'LL BE ALL.

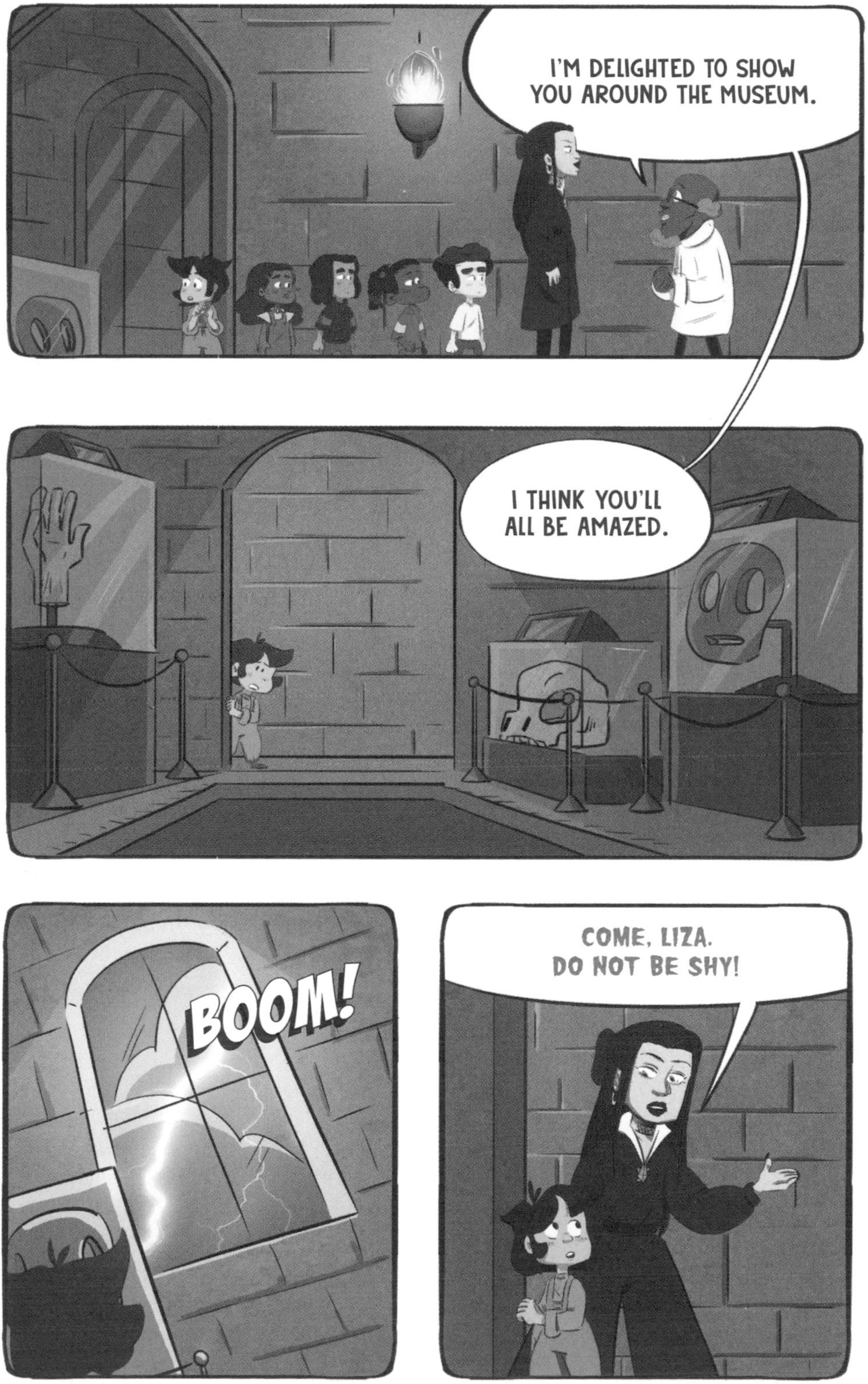
I'M DELIGHTED TO SHOW YOU AROUND THE MUSEUM.
I THINK YOU'LL ALL BE AMAZED.
BOOM!
COME, LIZA. DO NOT BE SHY!

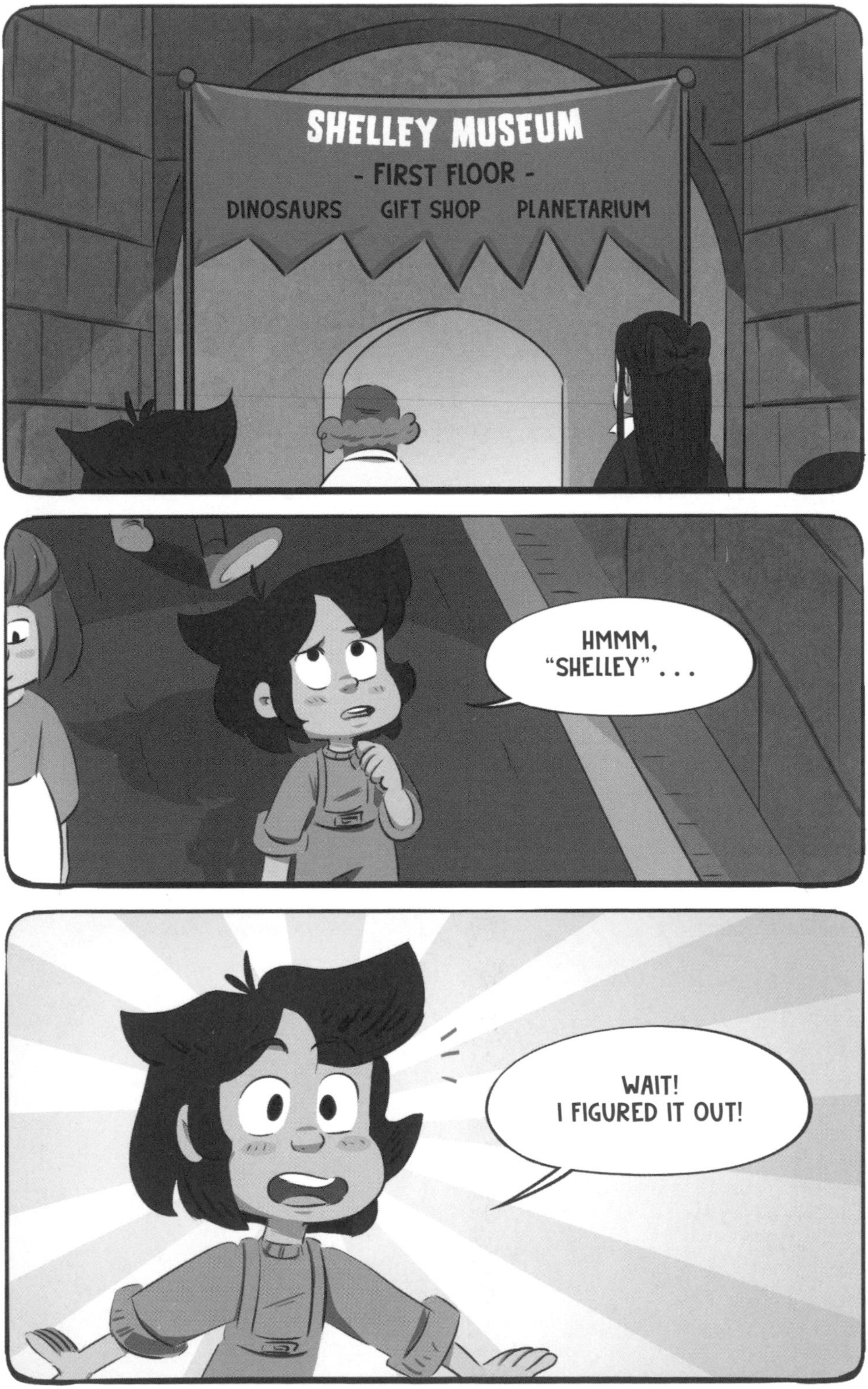
SHELLEY MUSEUM
- FIRST FLOOR -
DINOSAURS GIFT SHOP PLANETARIUM
HMMM, "SHELLEY" . . .
WAIT! I FIGURED IT OUT!

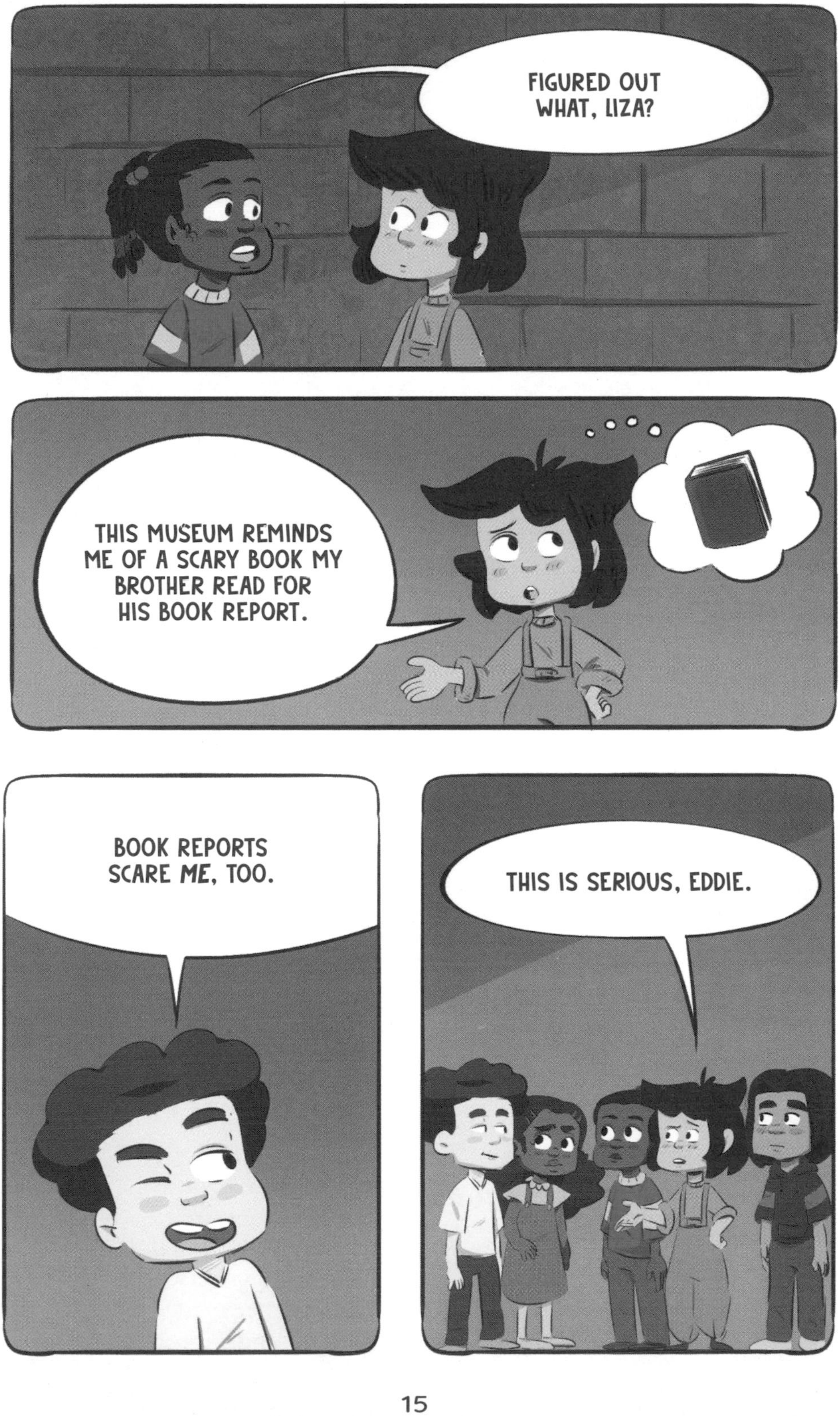
FIGURED OUT WHAT, LIZA?
THIS MUSEUM REMINDS ME OF A SCARY BOOK MY BROTHER READ FOR HIS BOOK REPORT.
BOOK REPORTS SCARE *ME*, TOO.
THIS IS SERIOUS, EDDIE.

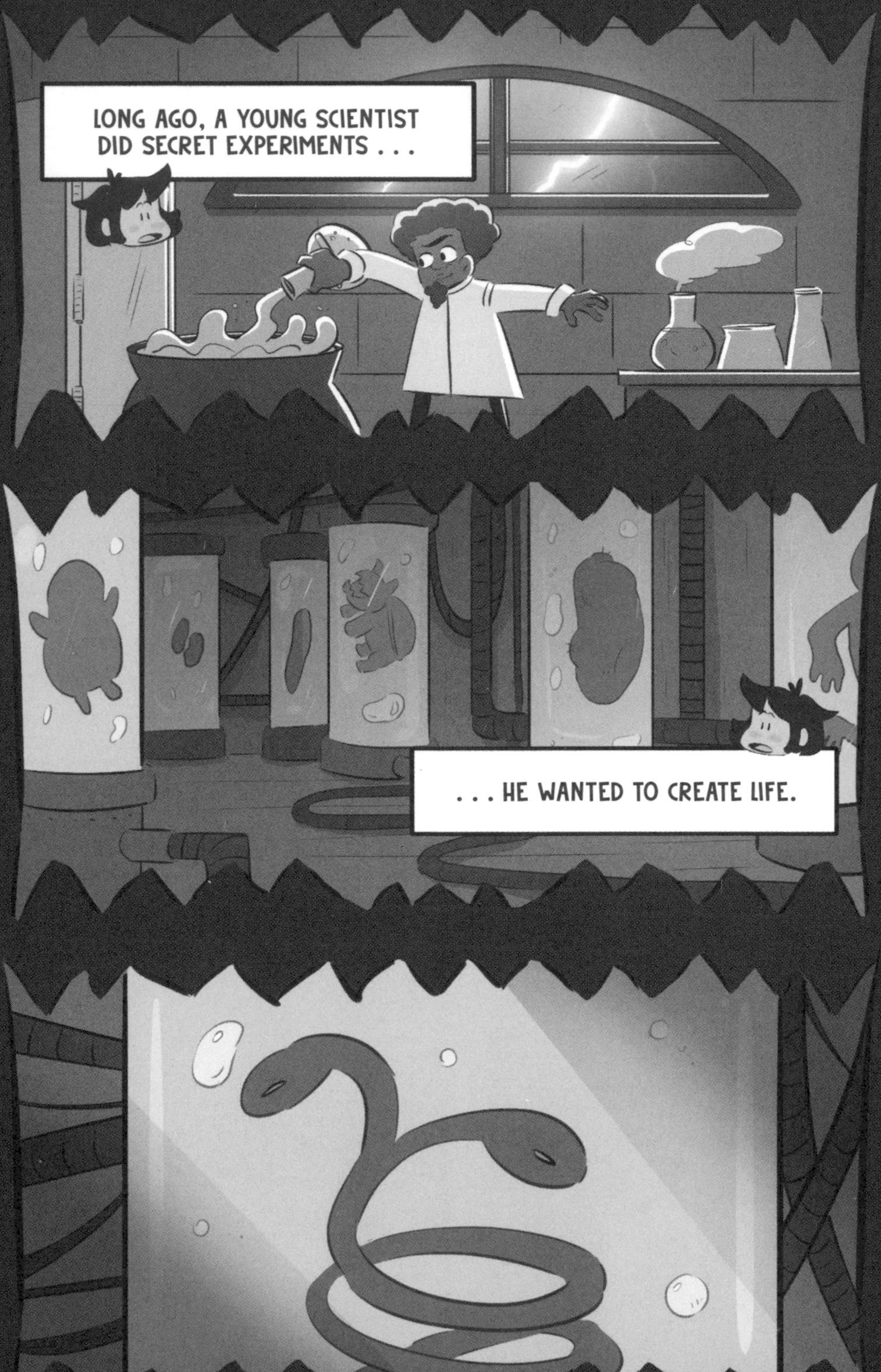
LONG AGO, A YOUNG SCIENTIST
DID SECRET EXPERIMENTS . . .
. . . HE WANTED TO CREATE LIFE.

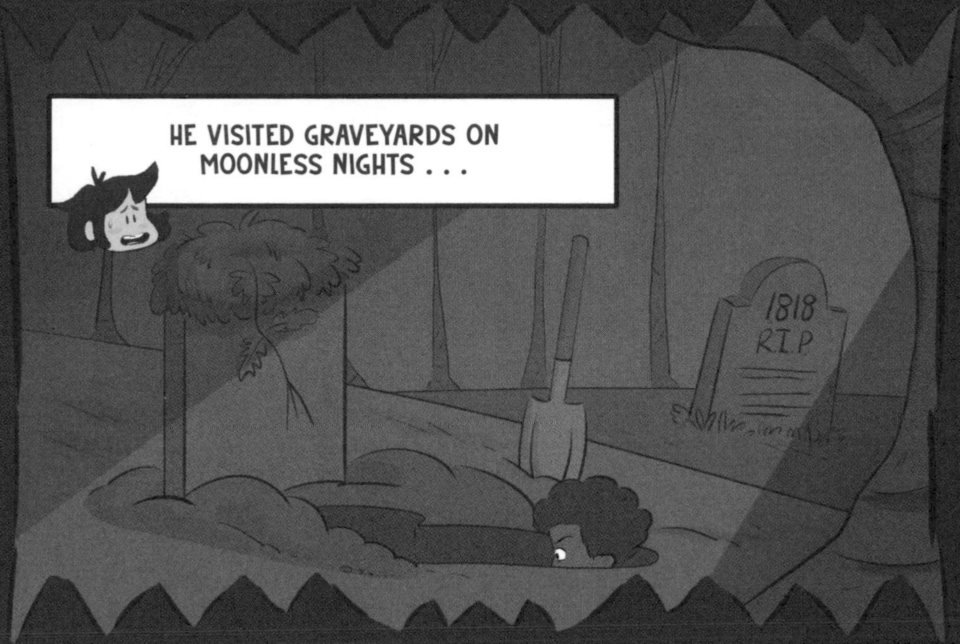
HE VISITED GRAVEYARDS ON MOONLESS NIGHTS . . .
1818 R.I.P.

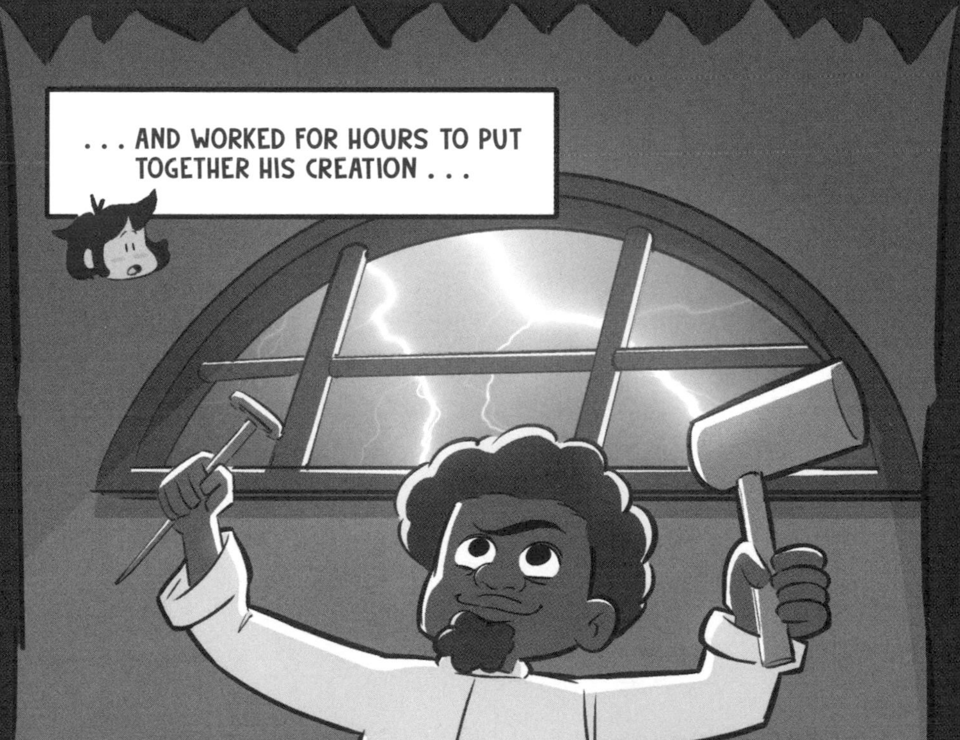
. . . AND WORKED FOR HOURS TO PUT TOGETHER HIS CREATION . . .

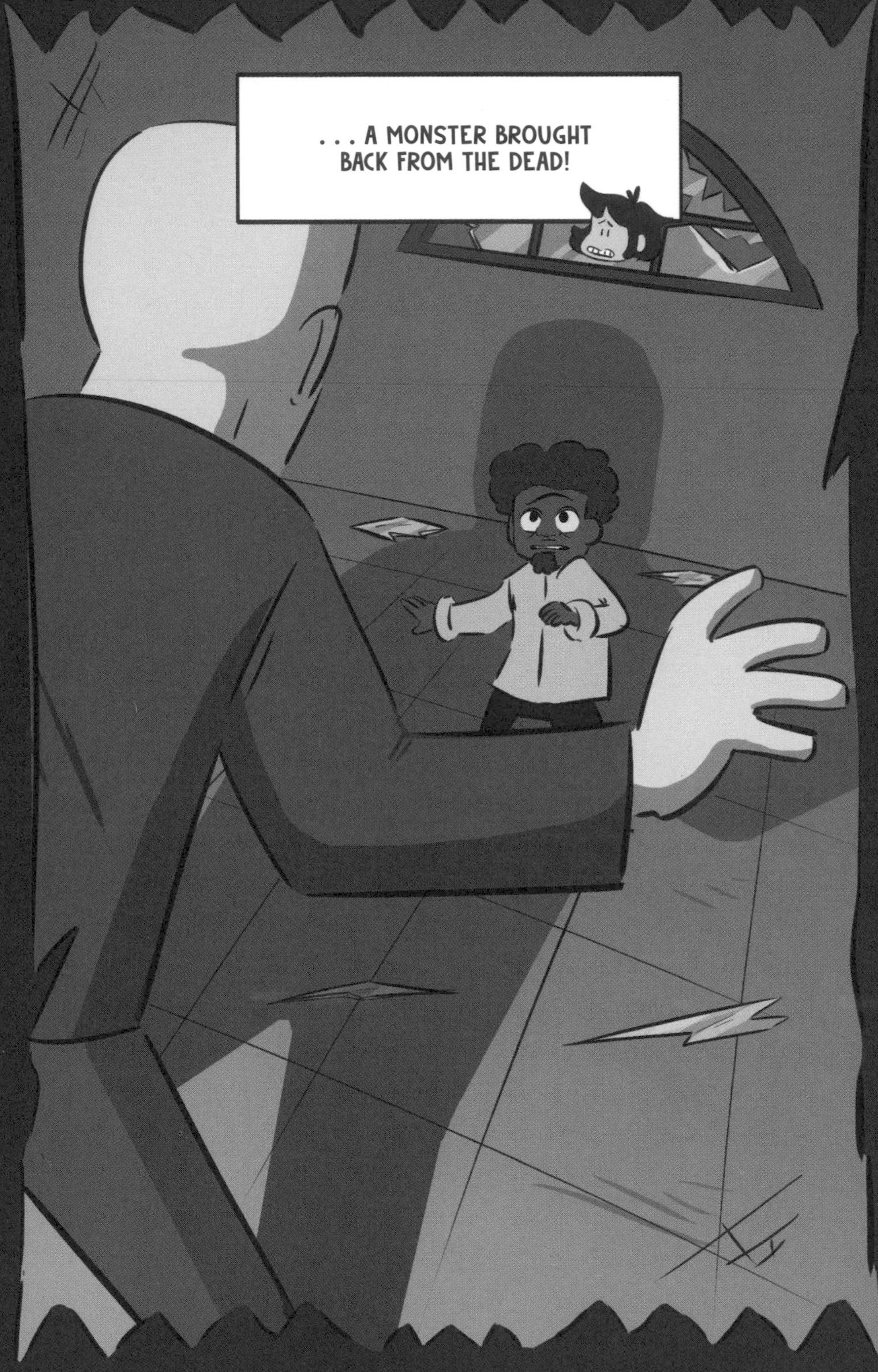
. . . A MONSTER BROUGHT
BACK FROM THE DEAD!

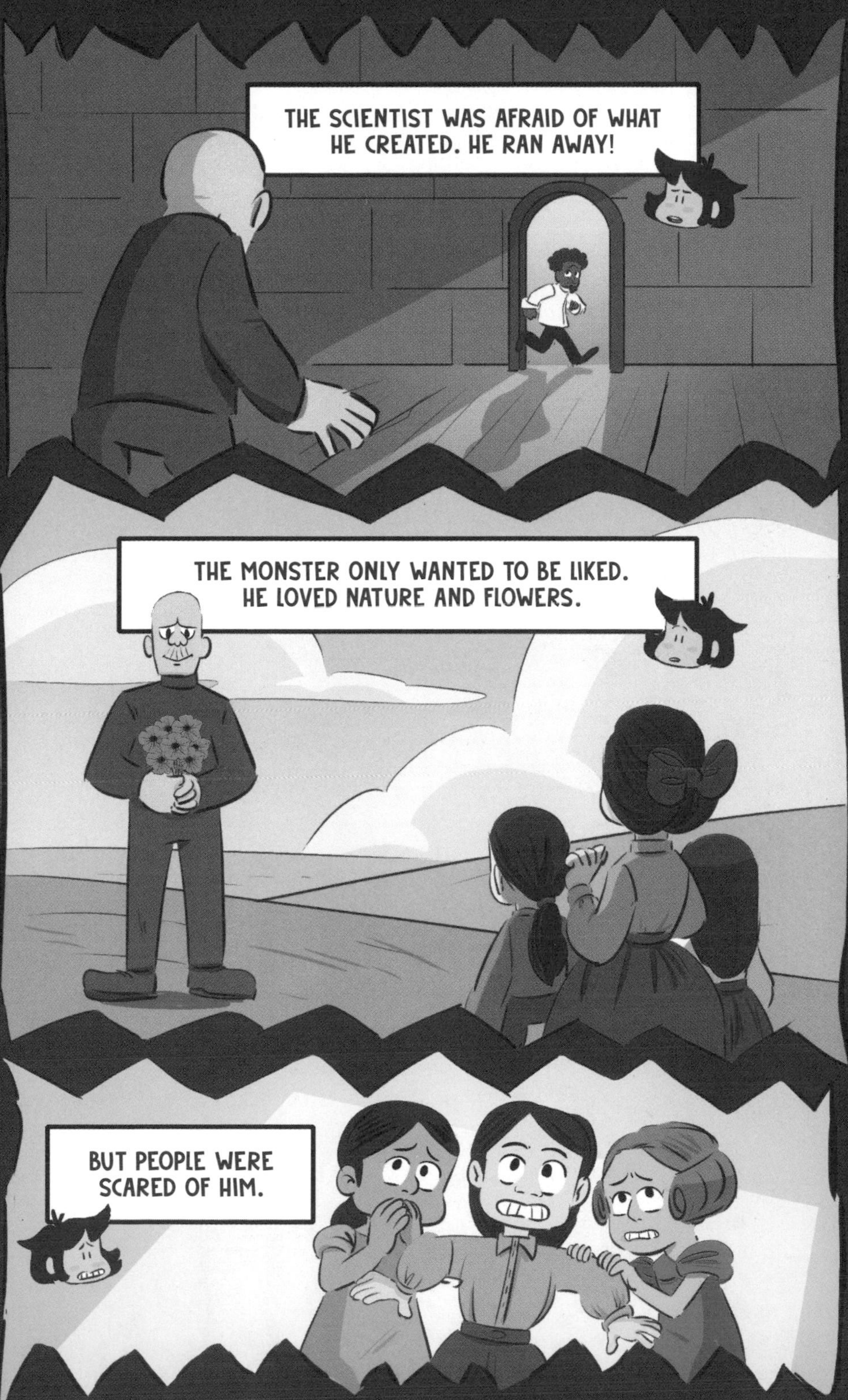
THE SCIENTIST WAS AFRAID OF WHAT HE CREATED. HE RAN AWAY!
THE MONSTER ONLY WANTED TO BE LIKED. HE LOVED NATURE AND FLOWERS.
BUT PEOPLE WERE SCARED OF HIM.

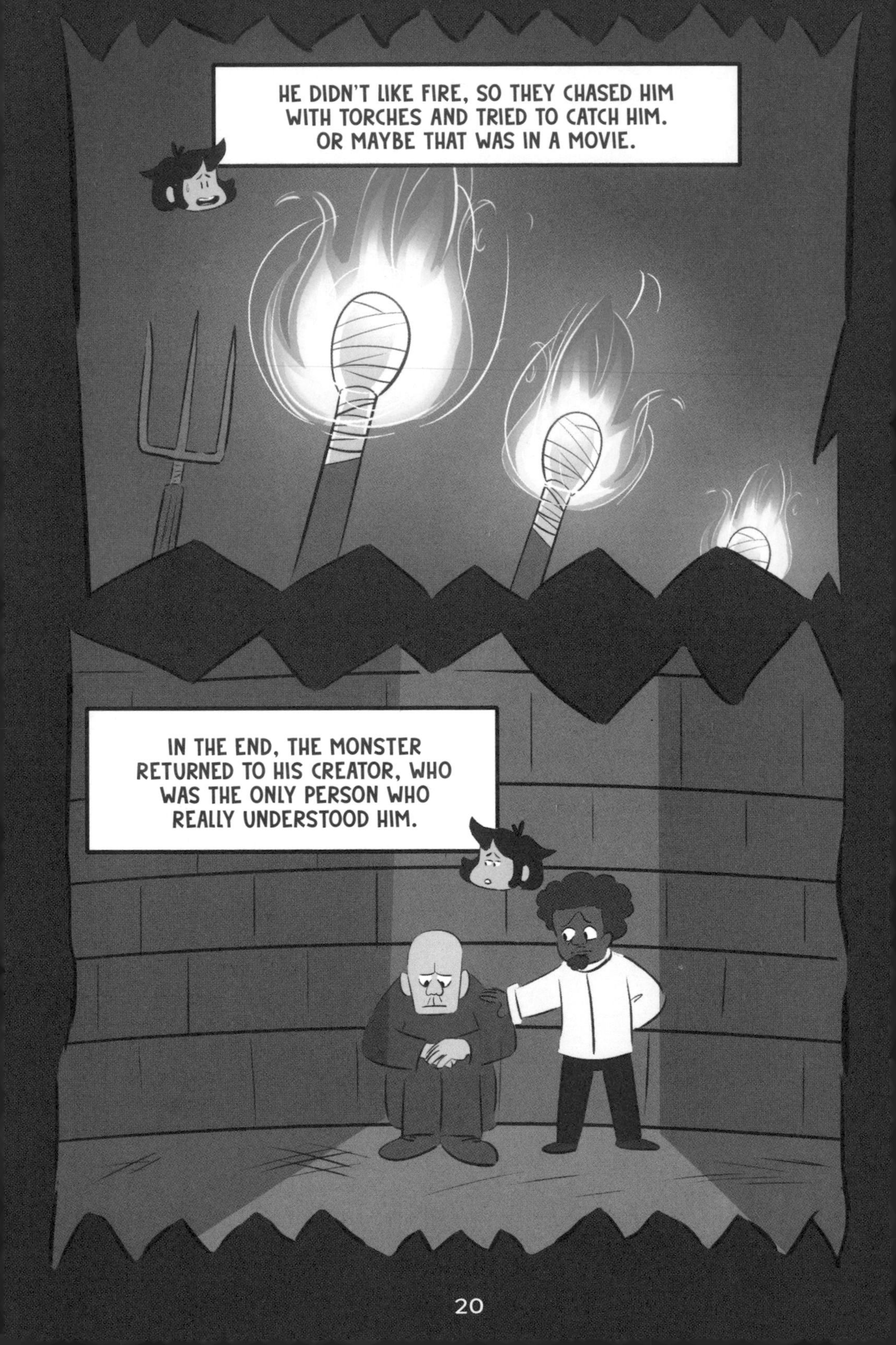
HE DIDN'T LIKE FIRE, SO THEY CHASED HIM WITH TORCHES AND TRIED TO CATCH HIM. OR MAYBE THAT WAS IN A MOVIE.
IN THE END, THE MONSTER RETURNED TO HIS CREATOR, WHO WAS THE ONLY PERSON WHO REALLY UNDERSTOOD HIM.

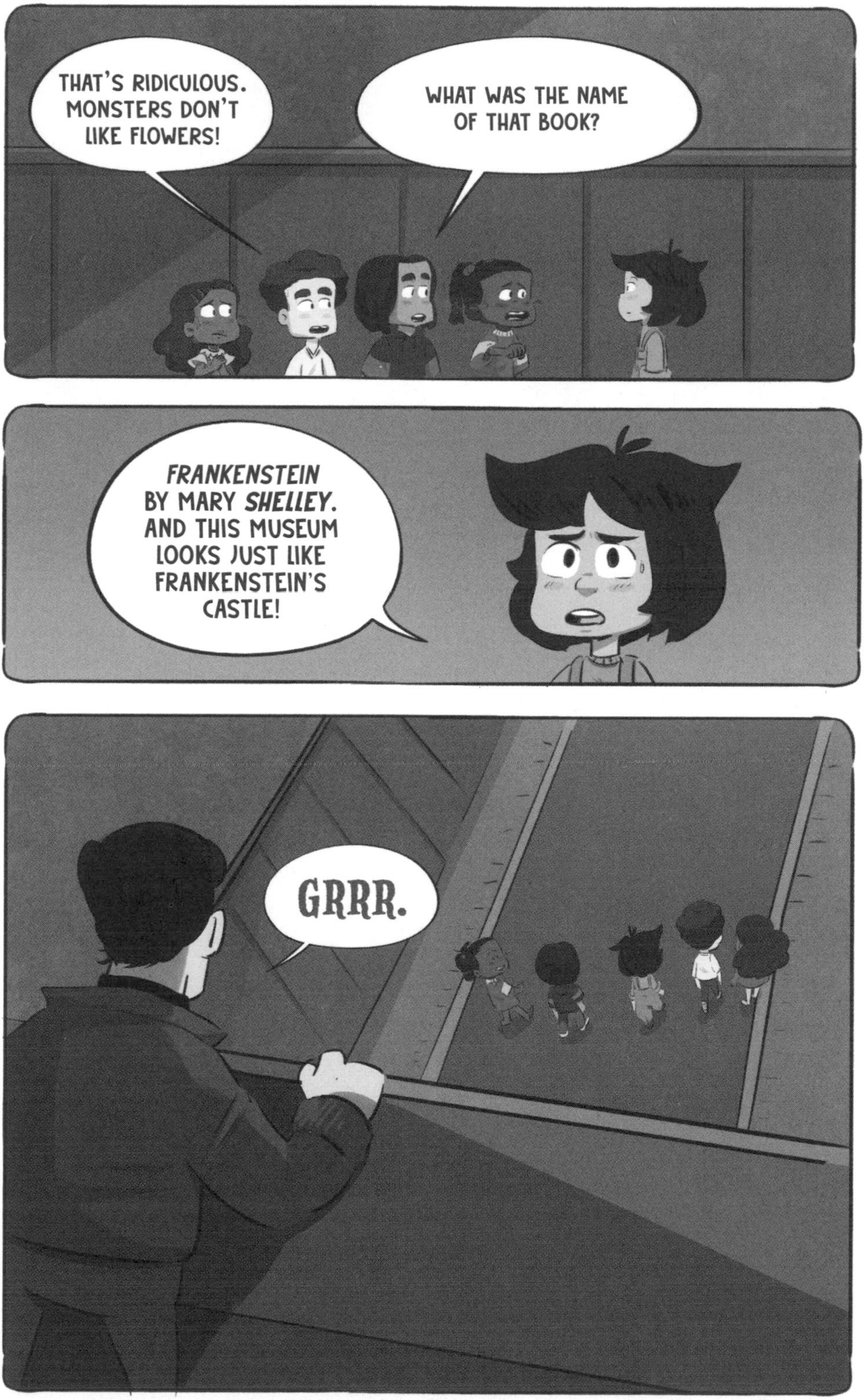
THAT'S RIDICULOUS. MONSTERS DON'T LIKE FLOWERS!
WHAT WAS THE NAME OF THAT BOOK?
FRANKENSTEIN BY MARY ***SHELLEY***. AND THIS MUSEUM LOOKS JUST LIKE FRANKENSTEIN'S CASTLE!
GRRR.

CHAPTER 3 THE LAB

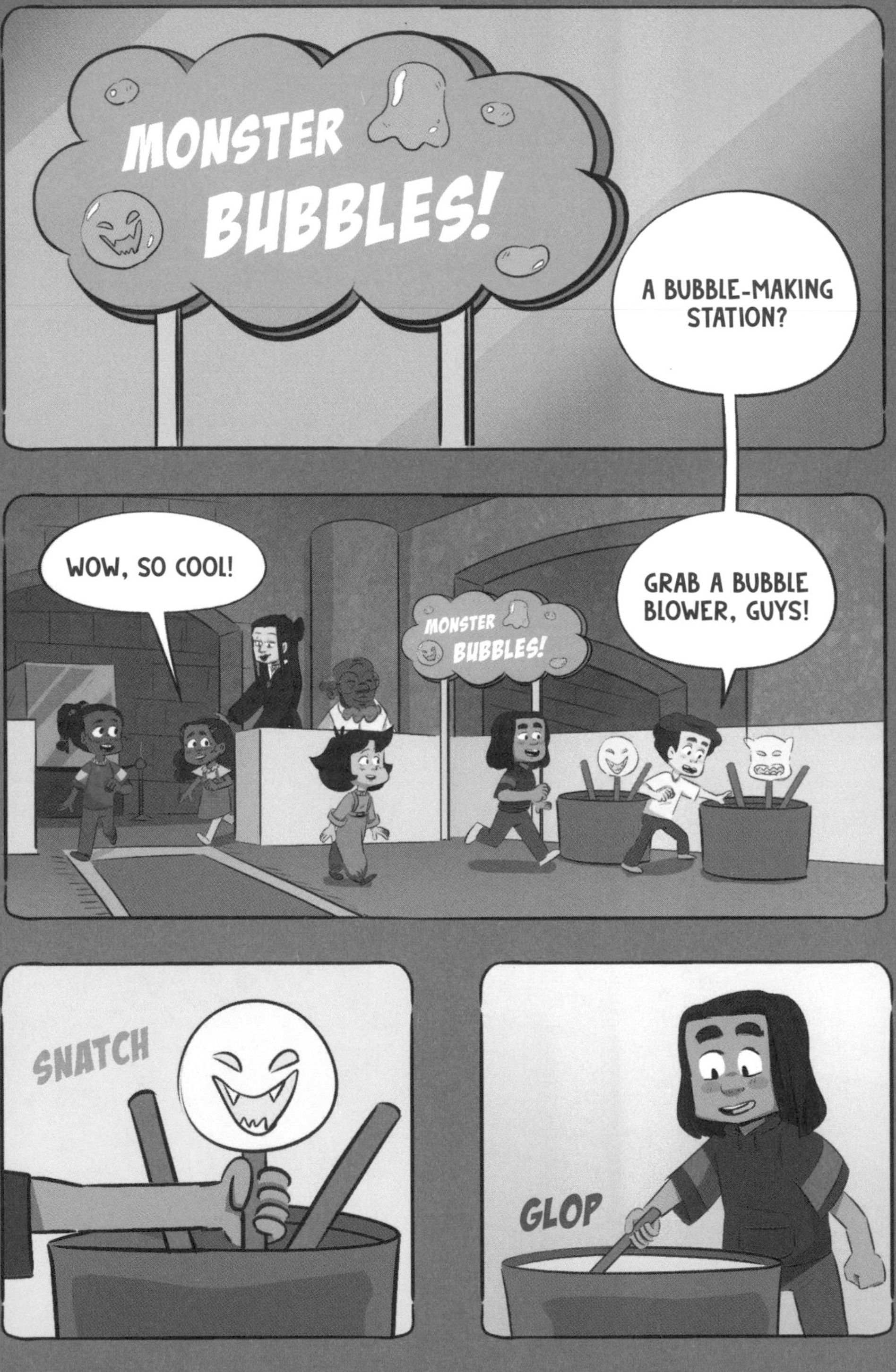
MONSTER BUBBLES!
A BUBBLE-MAKING STATION?
WOW, SO COOL!
MONSTER BUBBLES!
GRAB A BUBBLE BLOWER, GUYS!
SNATCH
GLOP

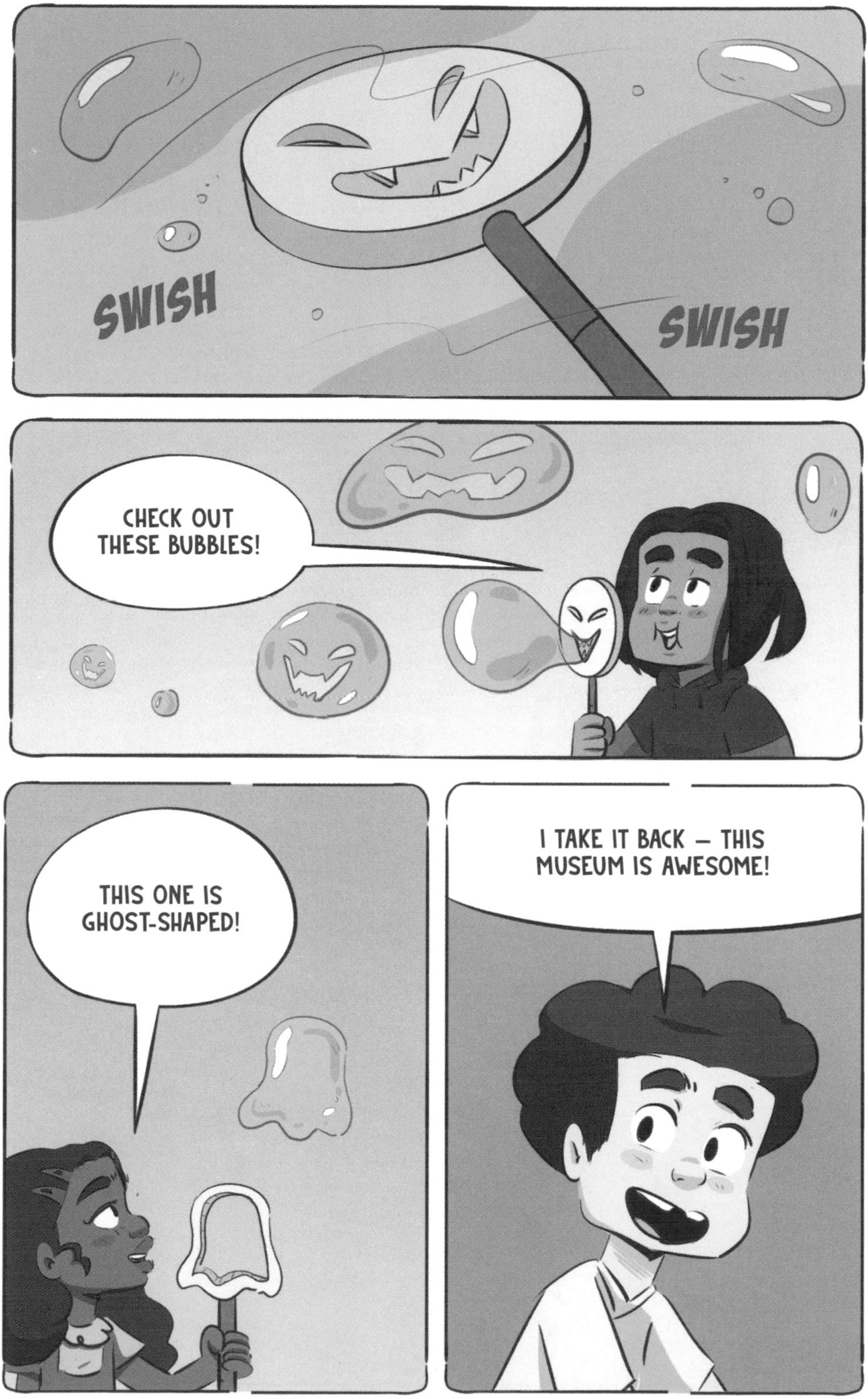
SWISH
SWISH
CHECK OUT THESE BUBBLES!
THIS ONE IS GHOST-SHAPED!
I TAKE IT BACK – THIS MUSEUM IS AWESOME!

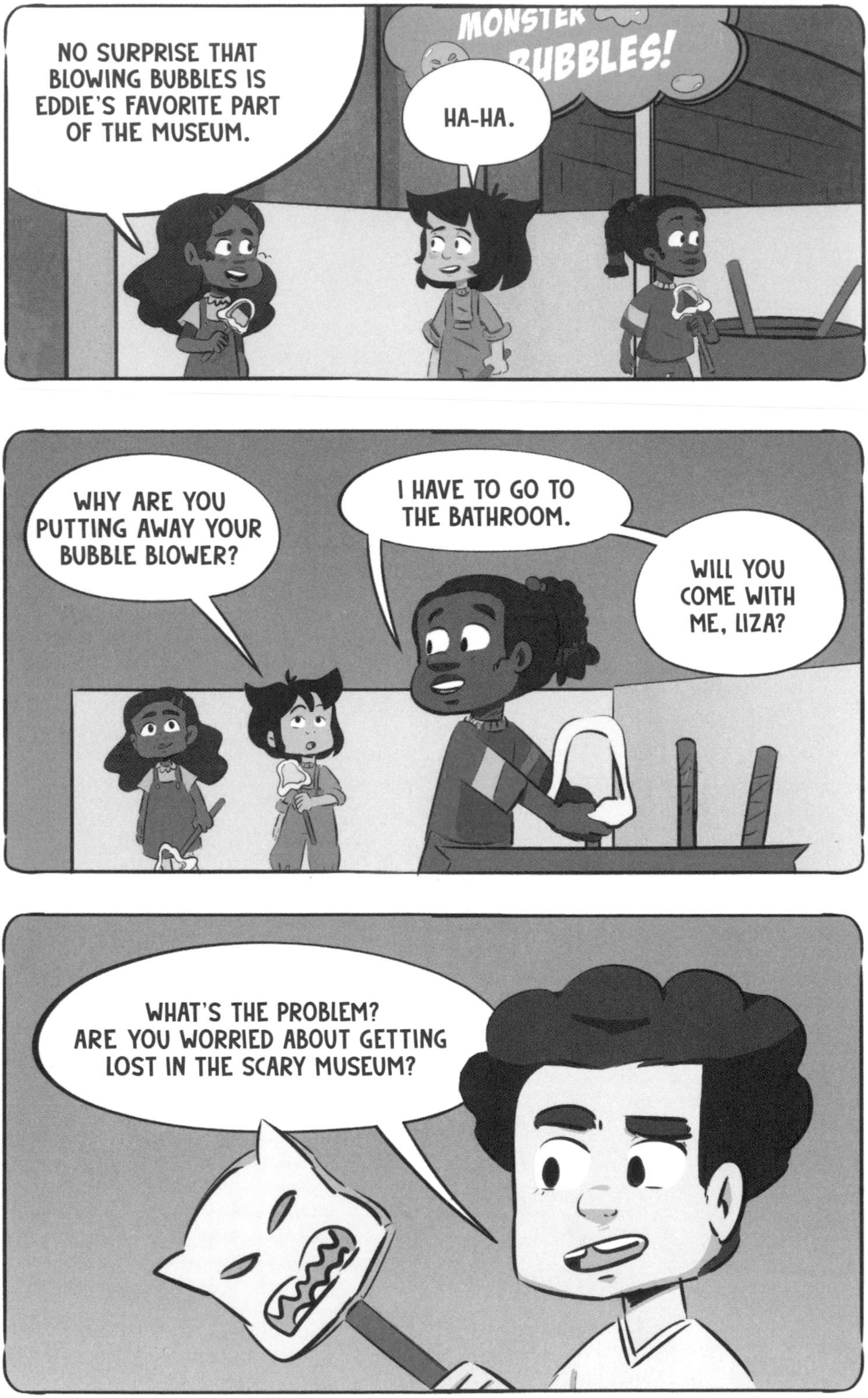
MONSTER BUBBLES!
NO SURPRISE THAT BLOWING BUBBLES IS EDDIE'S FAVORITE PART OF THE MUSEUM.
HA-HA.
WHY ARE YOU PUTTING AWAY YOUR BUBBLE BLOWER?
I HAVE TO GO TO THE BATHROOM.
WILL YOU COME WITH ME, LIZA?
WHAT'S THE PROBLEM? ARE YOU WORRIED ABOUT GETTING LOST IN THE SCARY MUSEUM?

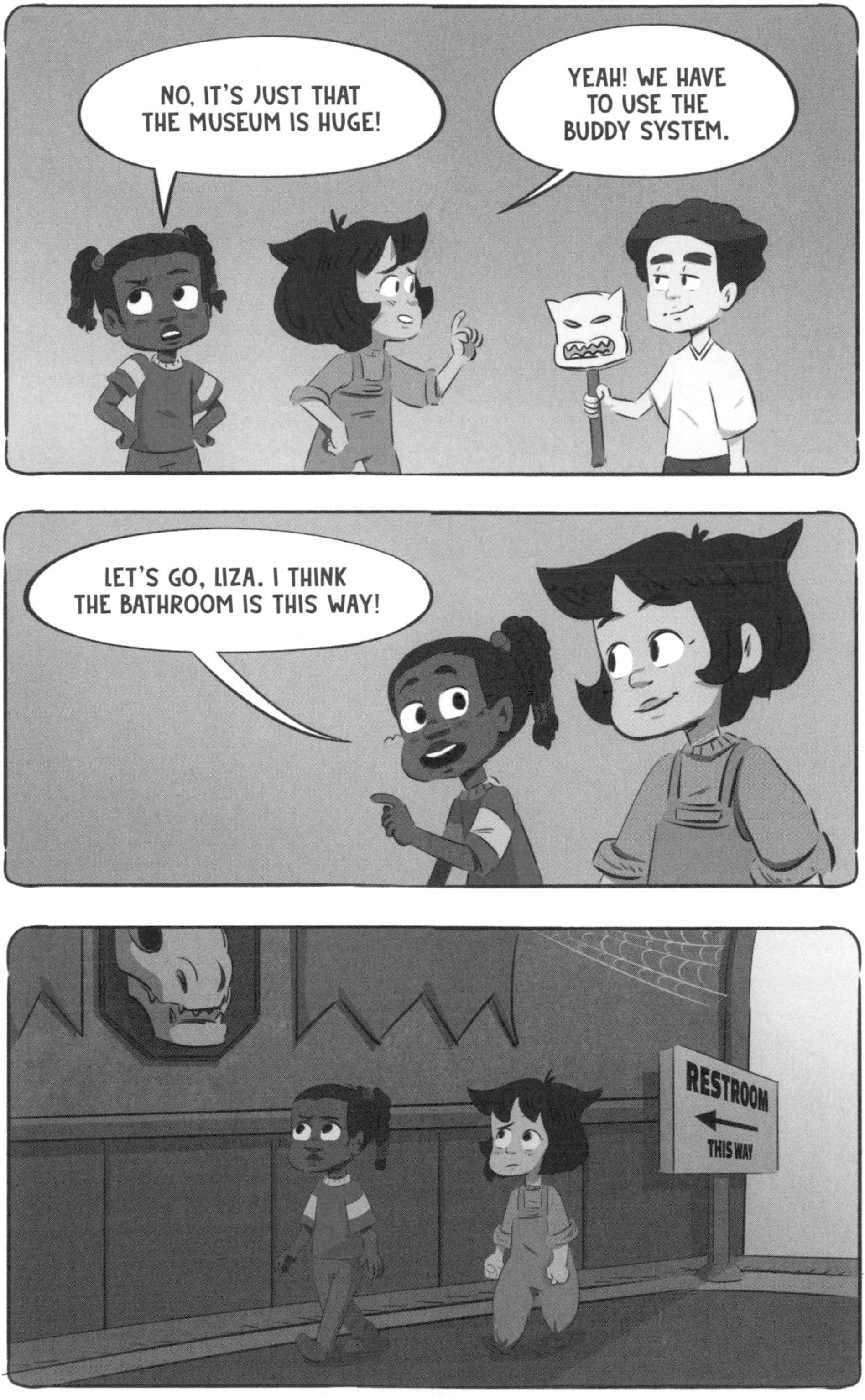
NO, IT'S JUST THAT THE MUSEUM IS HUGE!
YEAH! WE HAVE TO USE THE BUDDY SYSTEM.
LET'S GO, LIZA. I THINK THE BATHROOM IS THIS WAY!
RESTROOM
THIS WAY

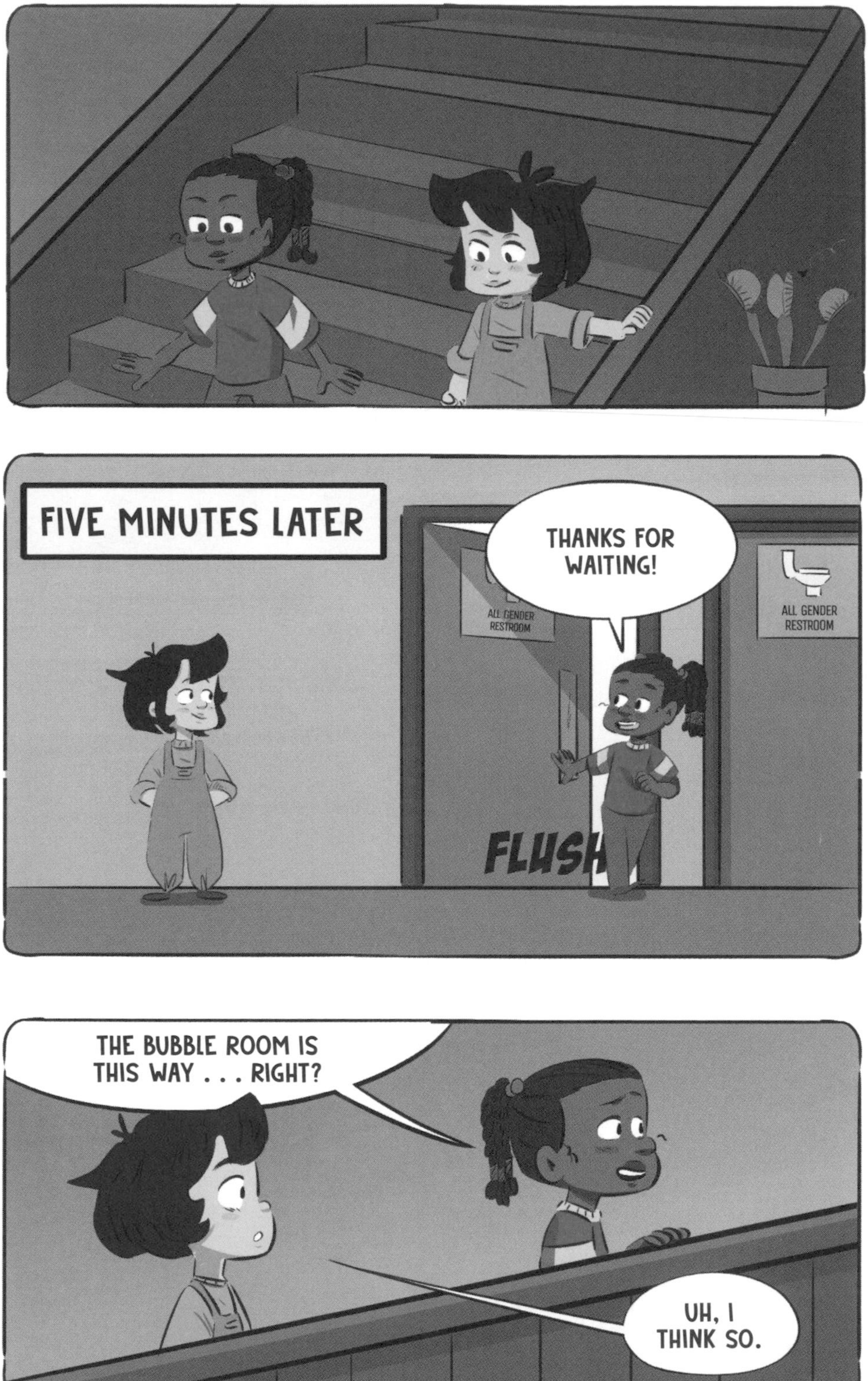
FIVE MINUTES LATER
THANKS FOR WAITING!
ALL GENDER RESTROOM
ALL GENDER RESTROOM
FLUSH
THE BUBBLE ROOM IS THIS WAY . . . RIGHT?
UH, I THINK SO.

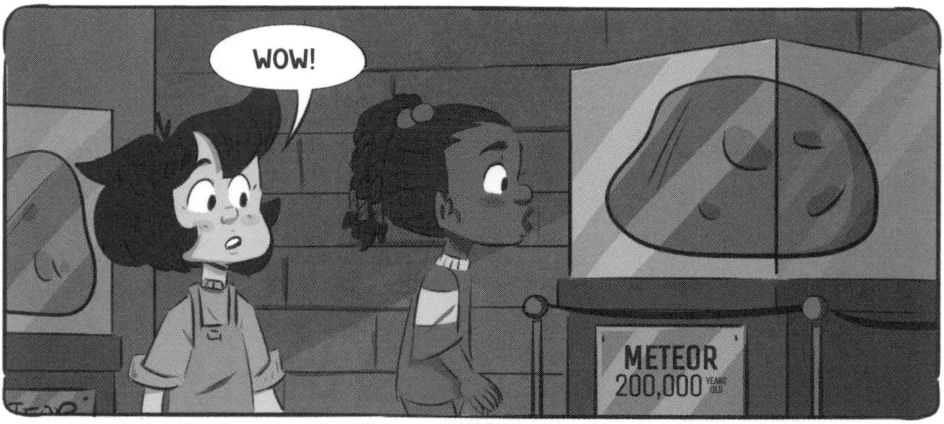
WOW!
METEOR
200,000 YEARS OLD

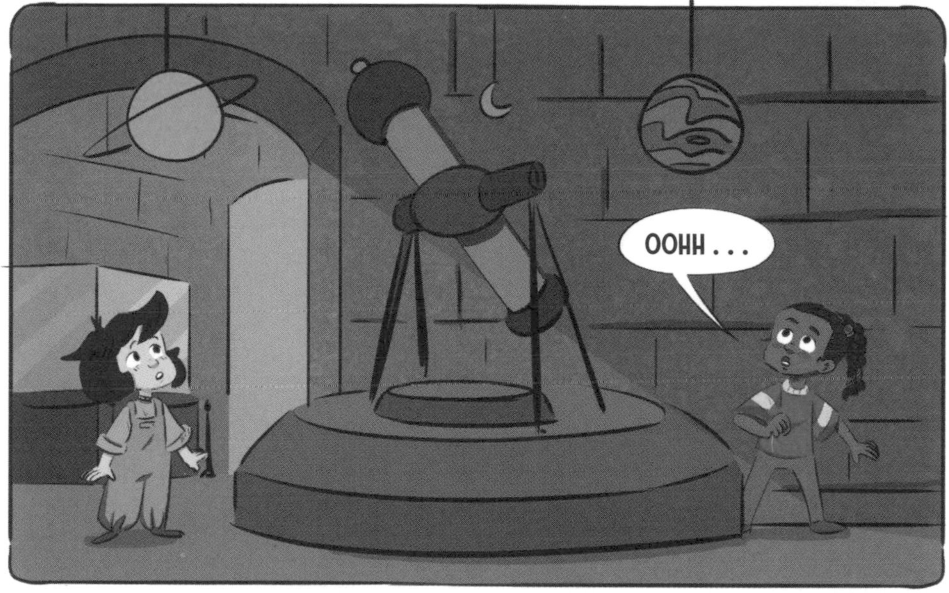
OOHH . . .

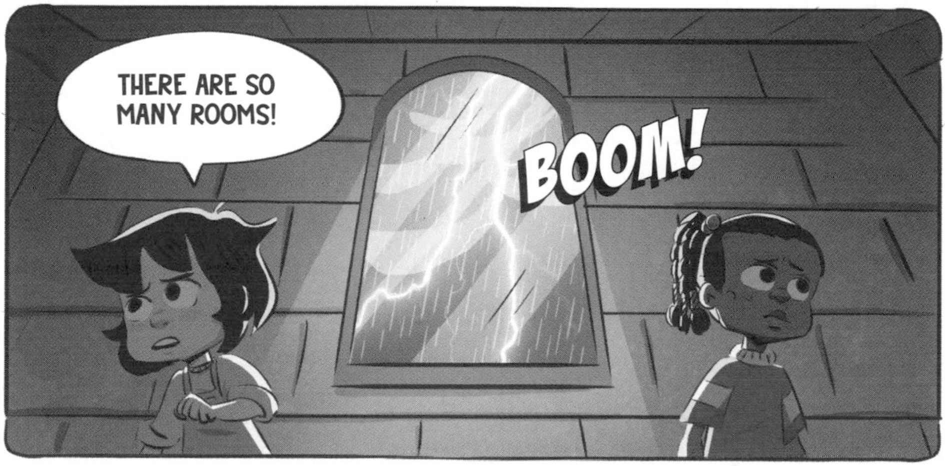
THERE ARE SO MANY ROOMS!
BOOM!

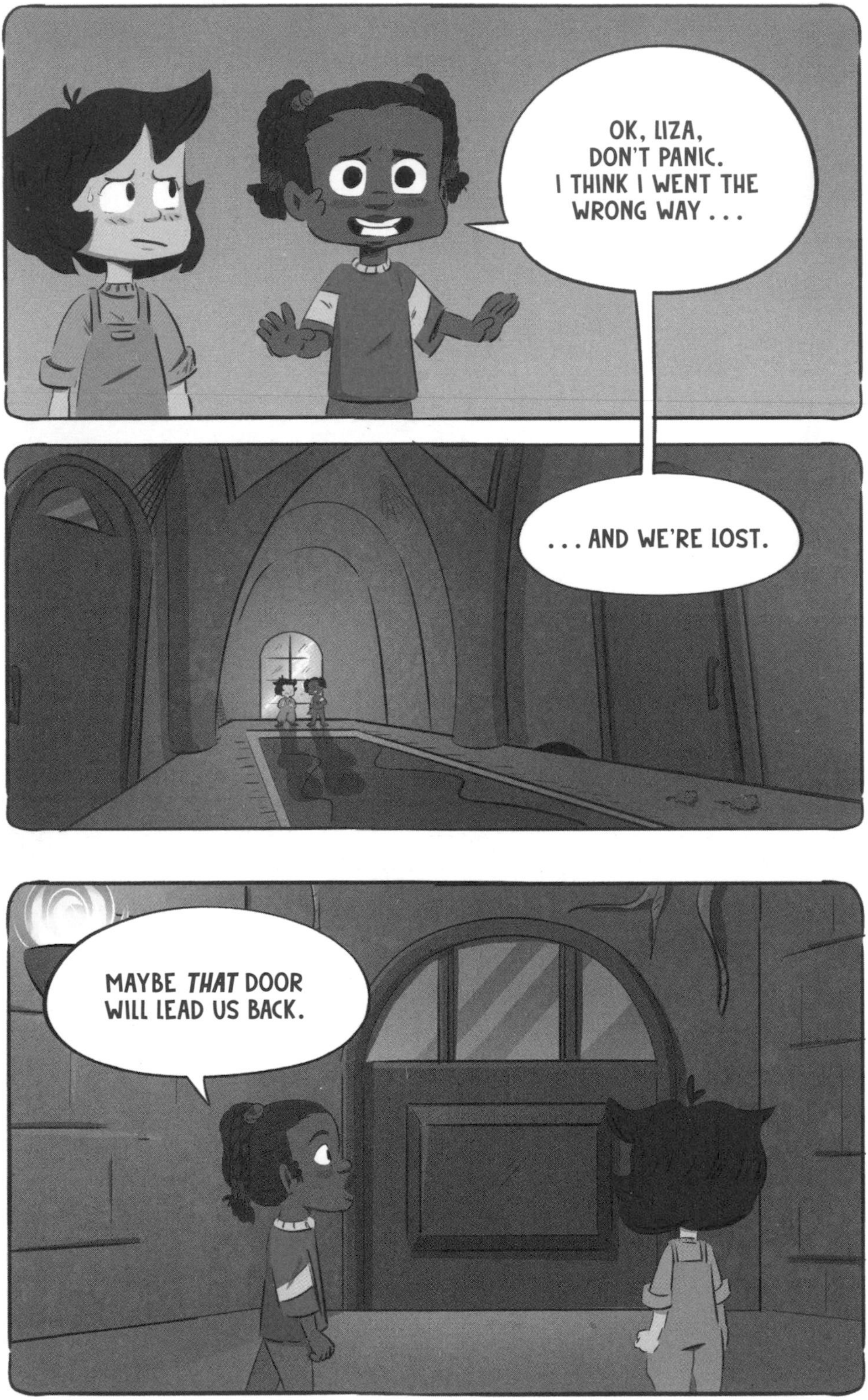
OK, LIZA, DON'T PANIC. I THINK I WENT THE WRONG WAY . . .
. . . AND WE'RE LOST.
MAYBE *THAT* DOOR WILL LEAD US BACK.

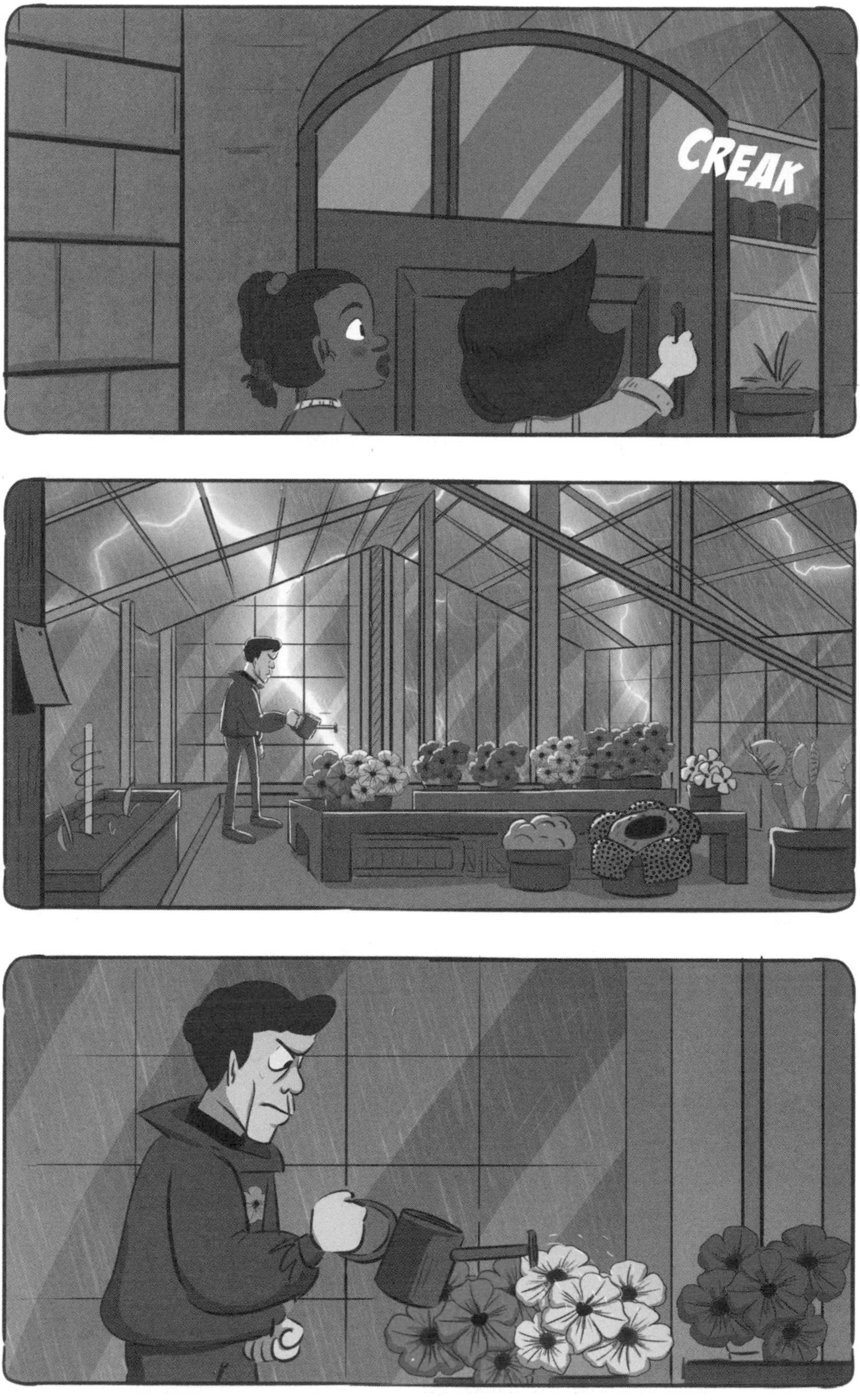
CREAK

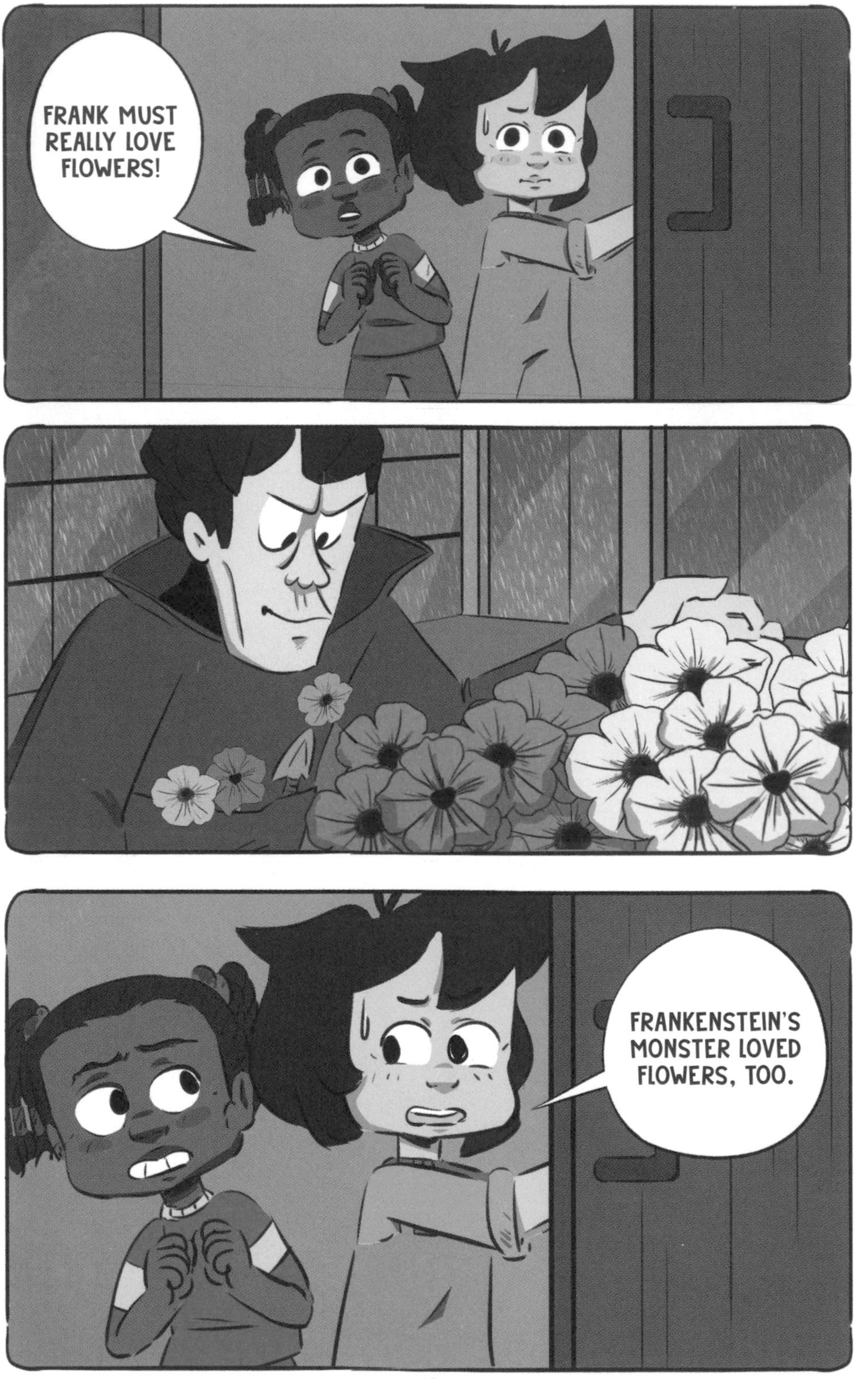
FRANK MUST REALLY LOVE FLOWERS!
FRANKENSTEIN'S MONSTER LOVED FLOWERS, TOO.

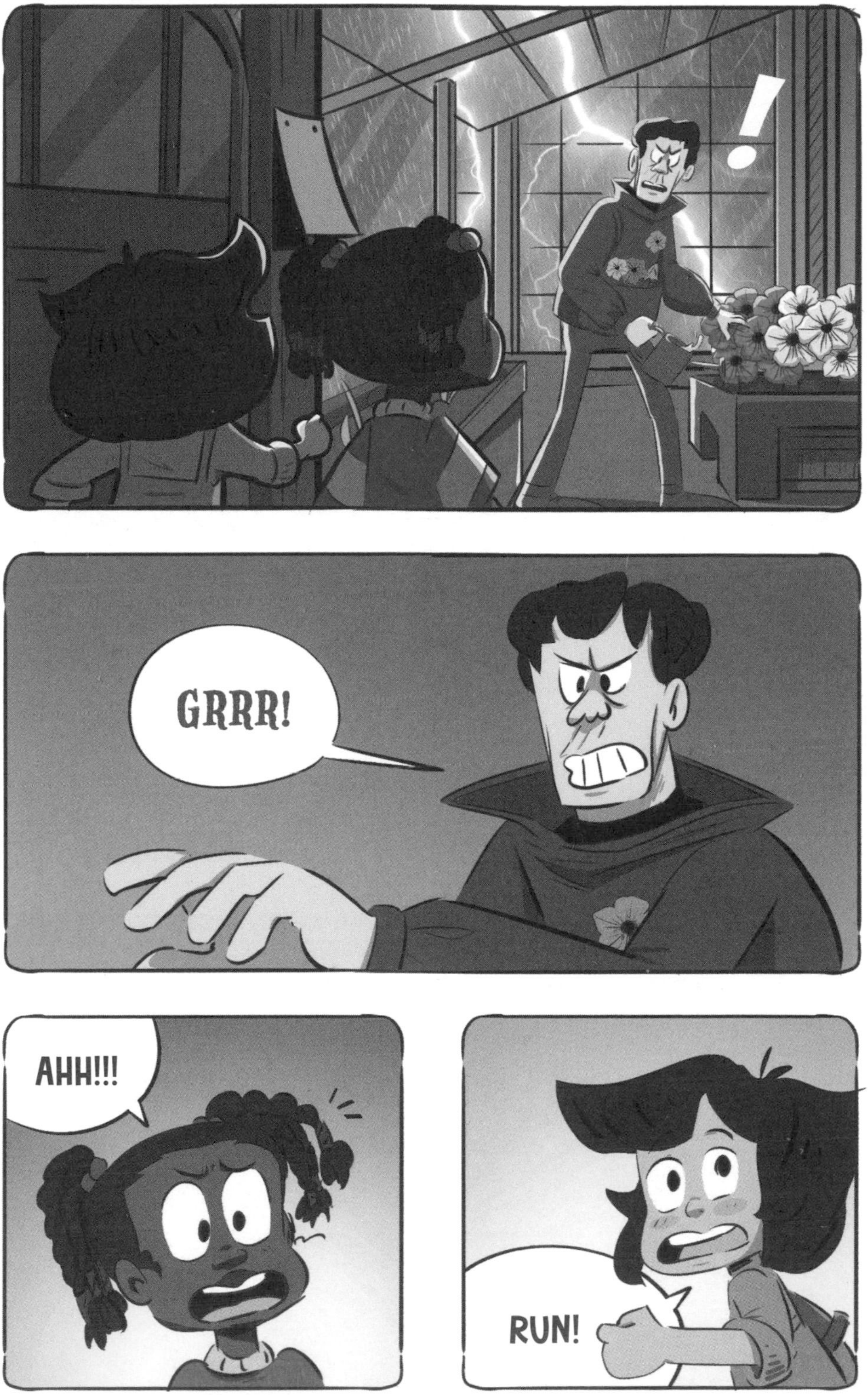
!
GRRR!
AHH!!!
RUN!

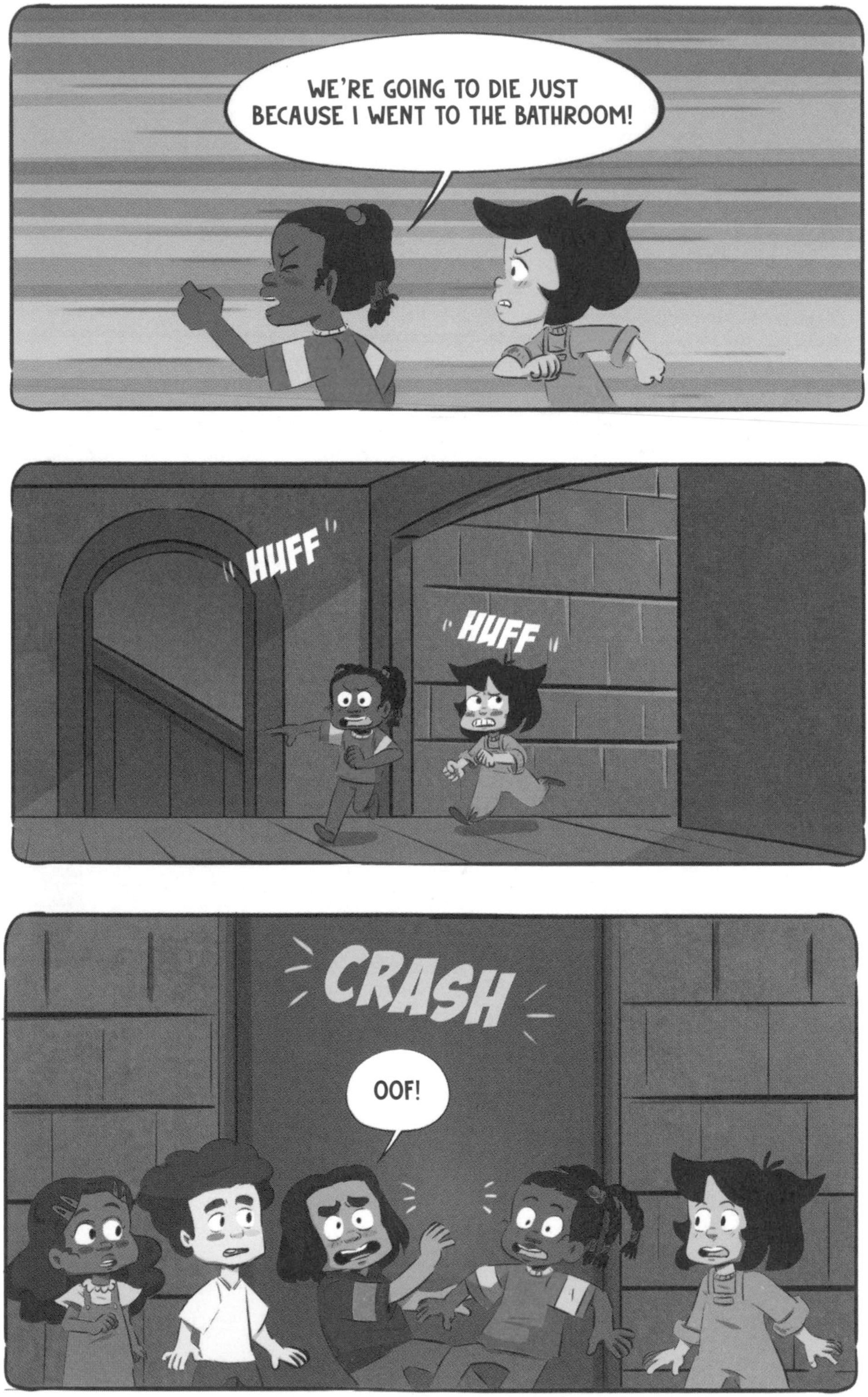
WE'RE GOING TO DIE JUST BECAUSE I WENT TO THE BATHROOM!
HUFF
HUFF
CRASH
OOF!

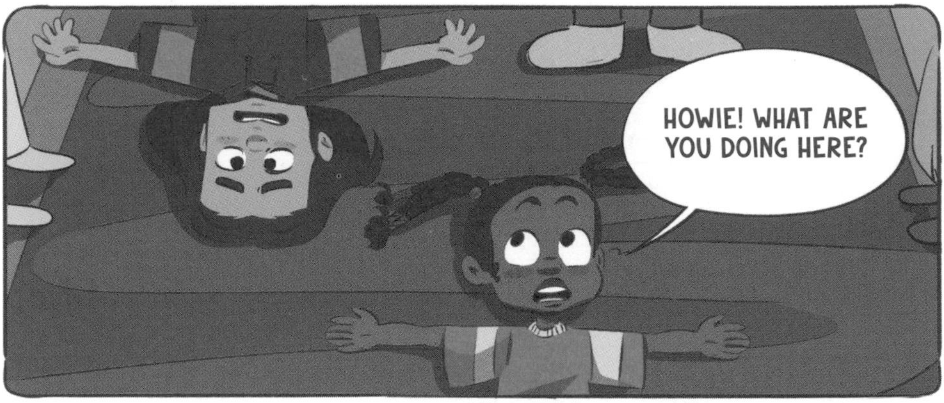
HOWIE! WHAT ARE YOU DOING HERE?

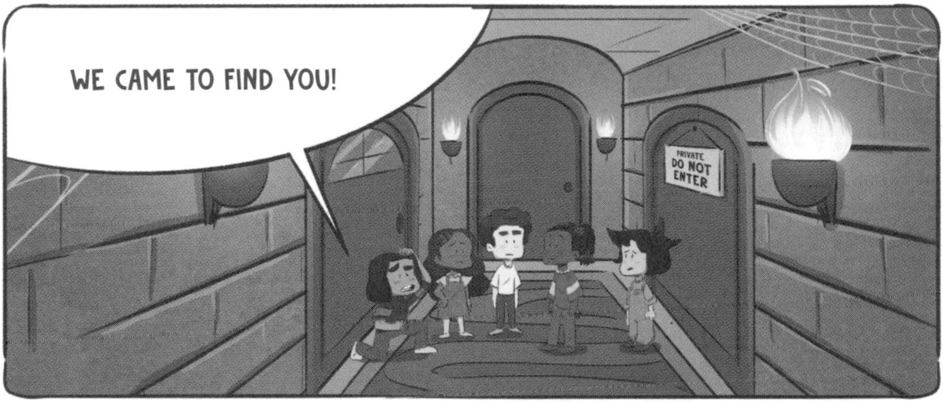
WE CAME TO FIND YOU!
PRIVATE DO NOT ENTER

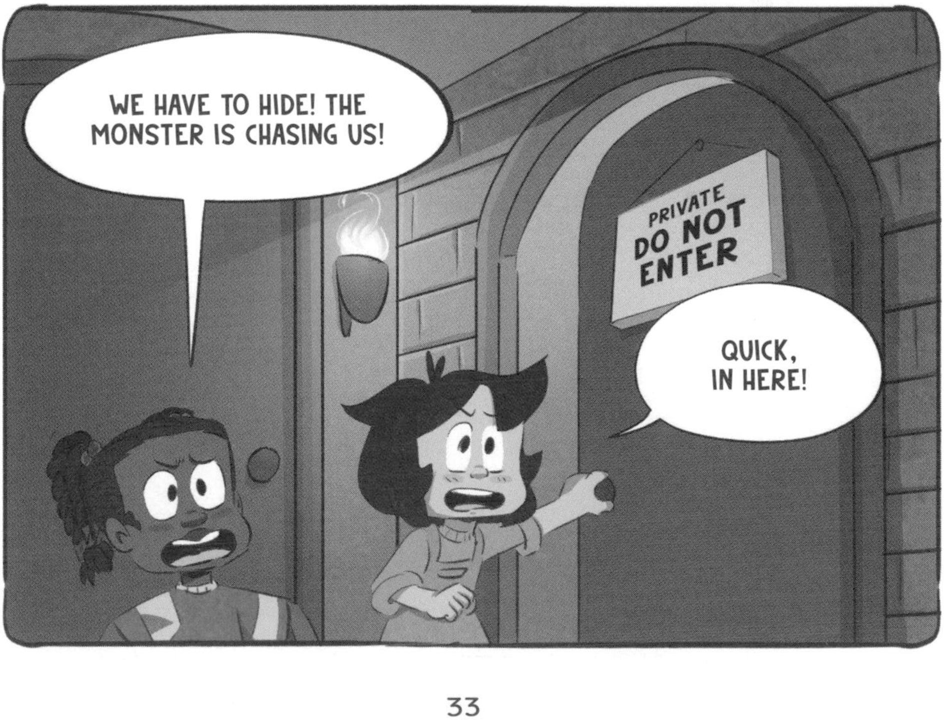
WE HAVE TO HIDE! THE MONSTER IS CHASING US!
PRIVATE DO NOT ENTER
QUICK, IN HERE!

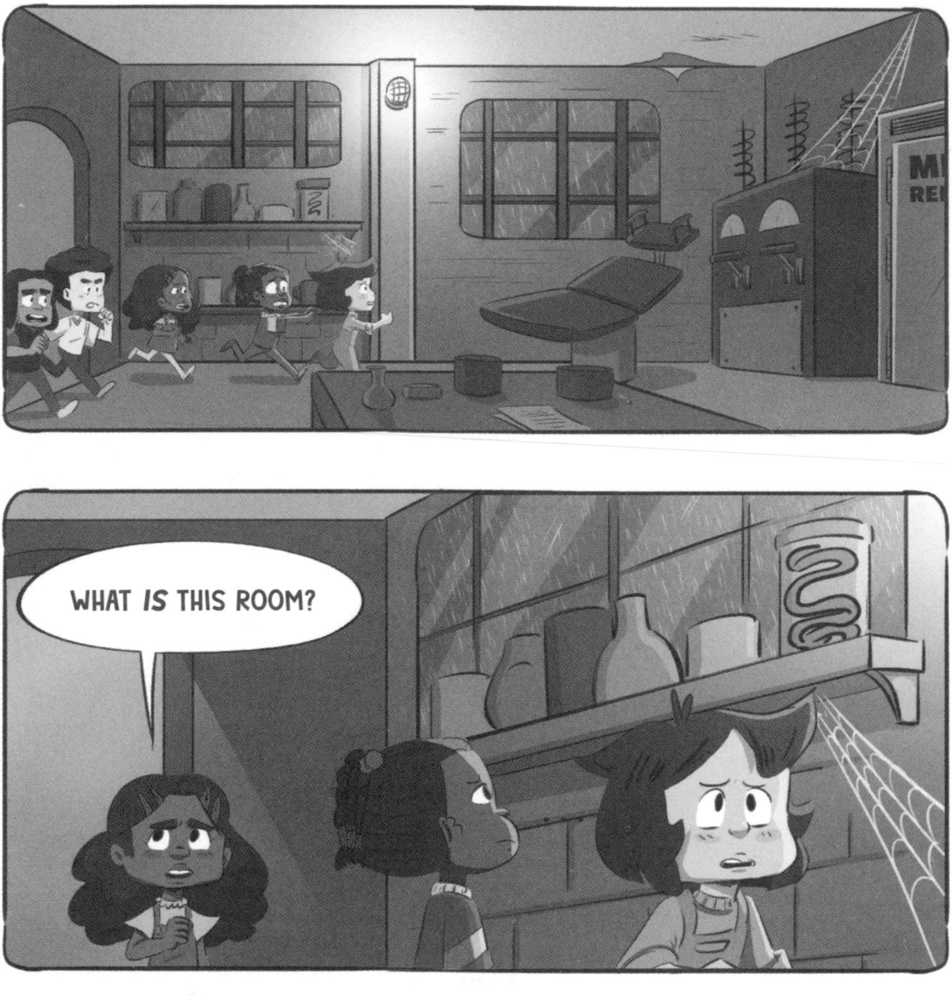
WHAT *IS* THIS ROOM?
THESE GLASS BEAKERS ARE JUST LIKE THE ONES IN MY DAD'S CHEMISTRY LAB.

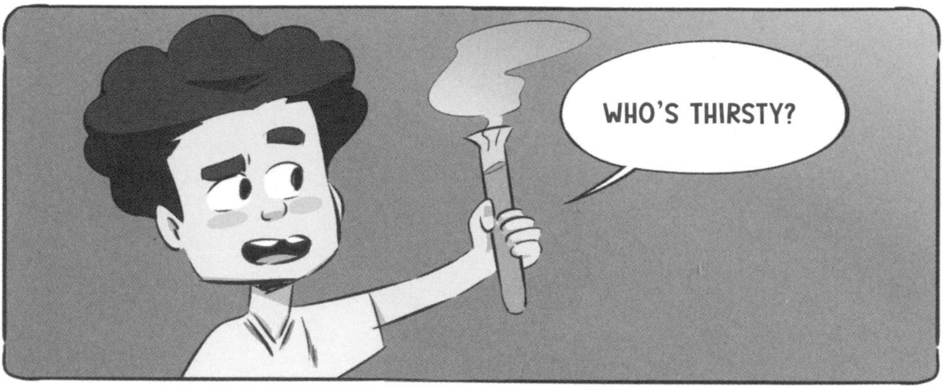
WHO'S THIRSTY?

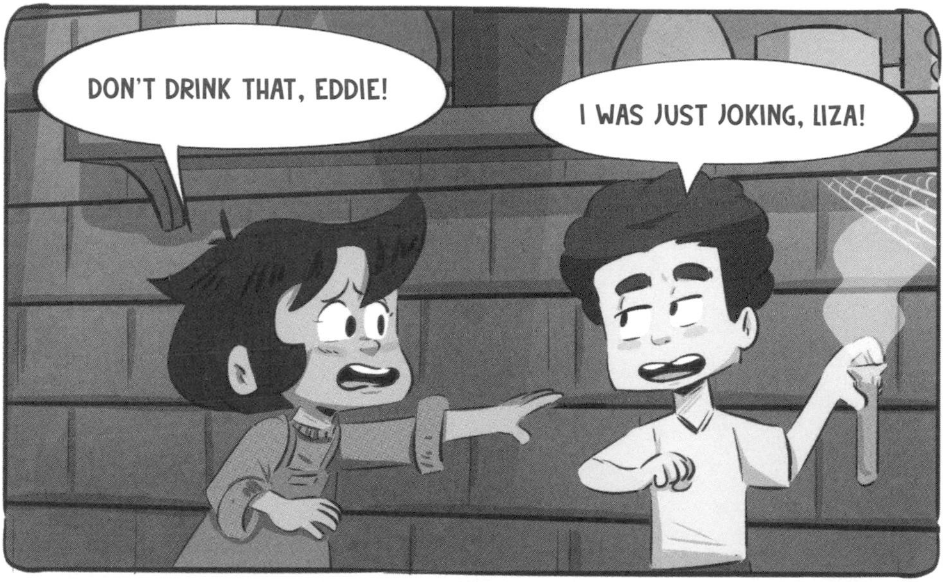
DON'T DRINK THAT, EDDIE!
I WAS JUST JOKING, LIZA!

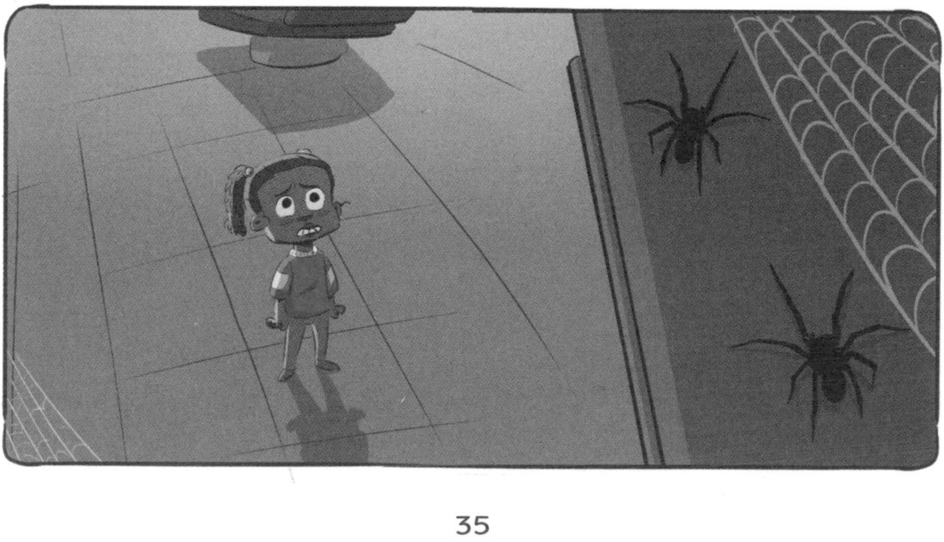

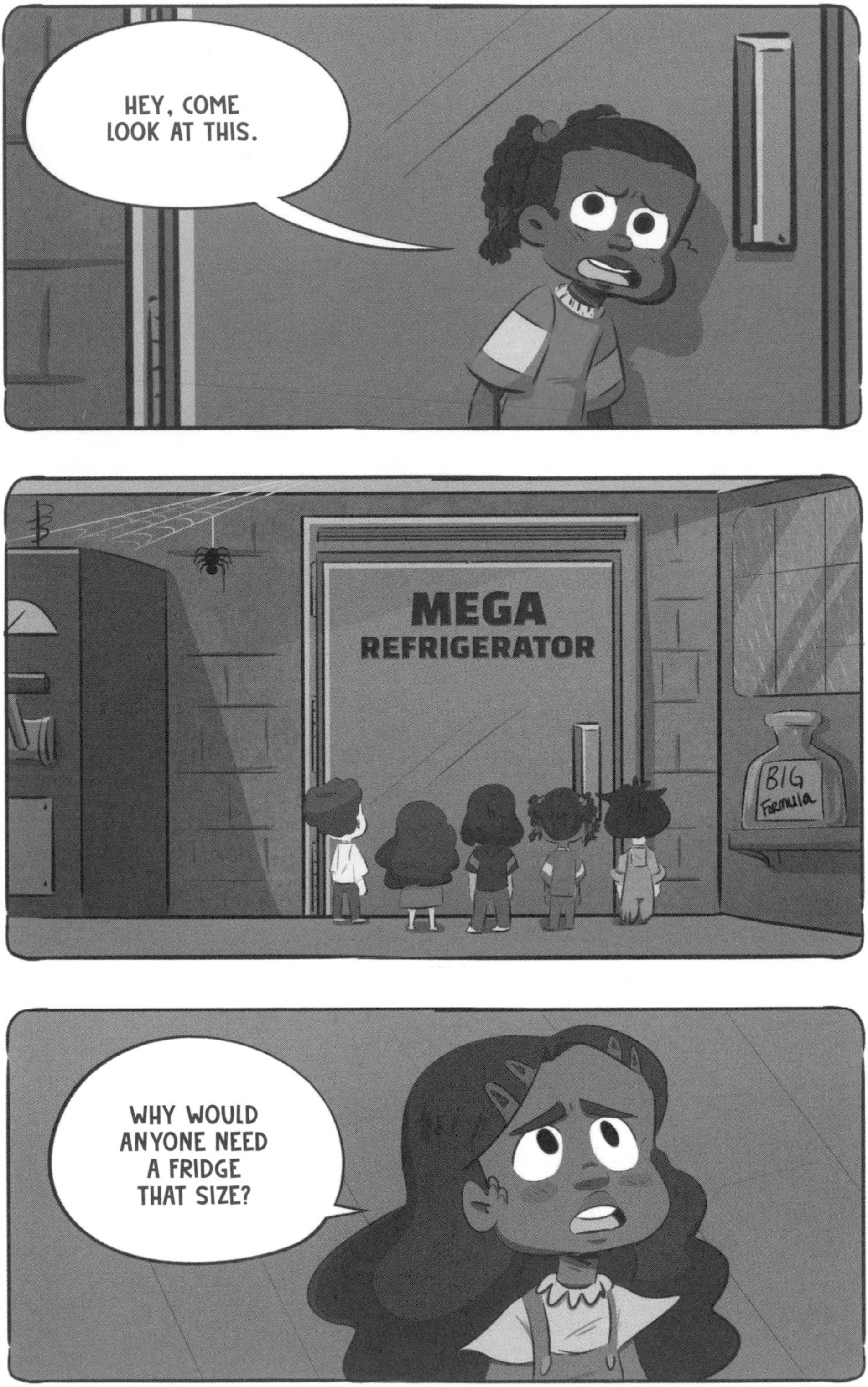
HEY, COME LOOK AT THIS.
MEGA REFRIGERATOR
BIG Formula
WHY WOULD ANYONE NEED A FRIDGE THAT SIZE?

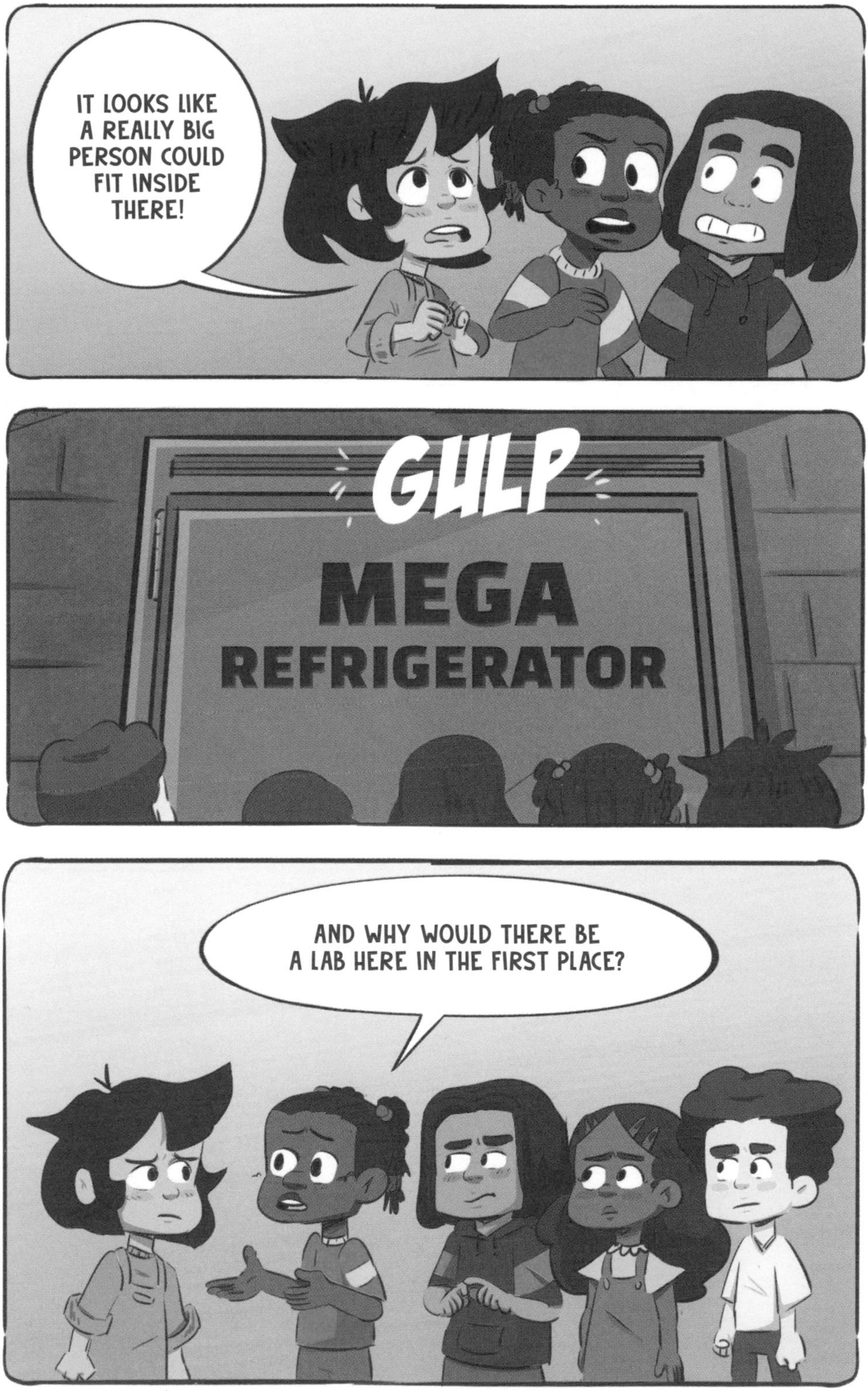
IT LOOKS LIKE A REALLY BIG PERSON COULD FIT INSIDE THERE!
GULP
MEGA REFRIGERATOR
AND WHY WOULD THERE BE A LAB HERE IN THE FIRST PLACE?

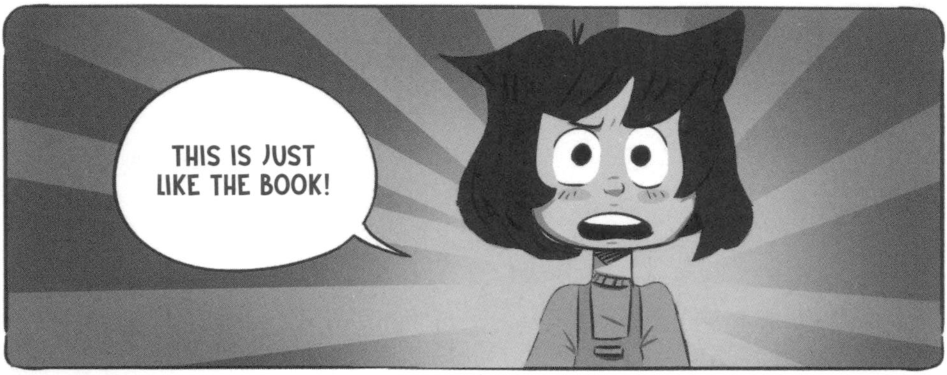
THIS IS JUST LIKE THE BOOK!

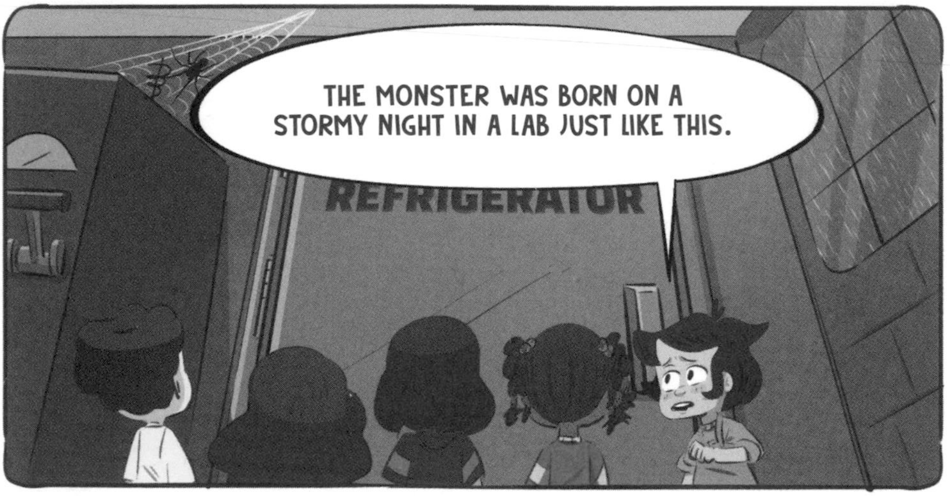
THE MONSTER WAS BORN ON A STORMY NIGHT IN A LAB JUST LIKE THIS.
REFRIGERATOR

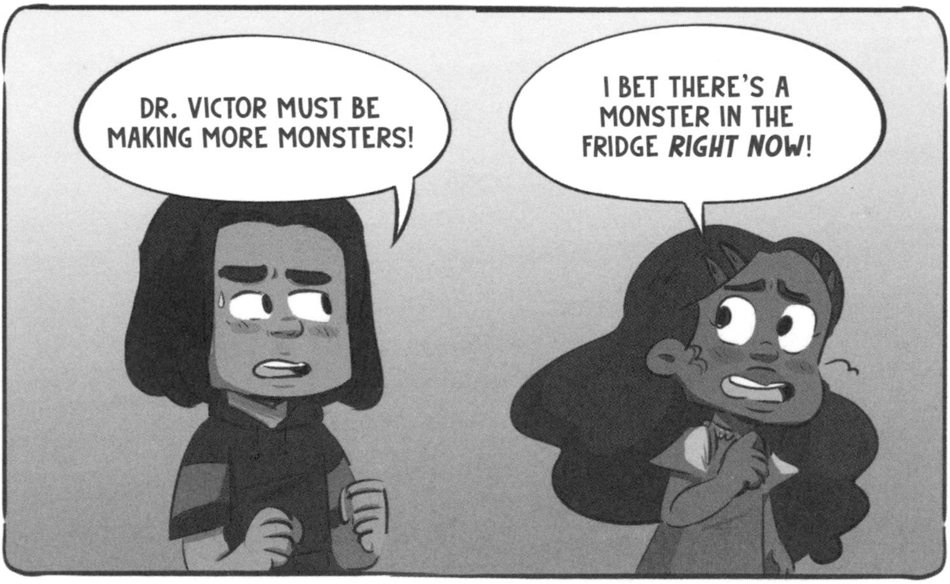
DR. VICTOR MUST BE MAKING MORE MONSTERS!
I BET THERE'S A MONSTER IN THE FRIDGE *RIGHT NOW*!

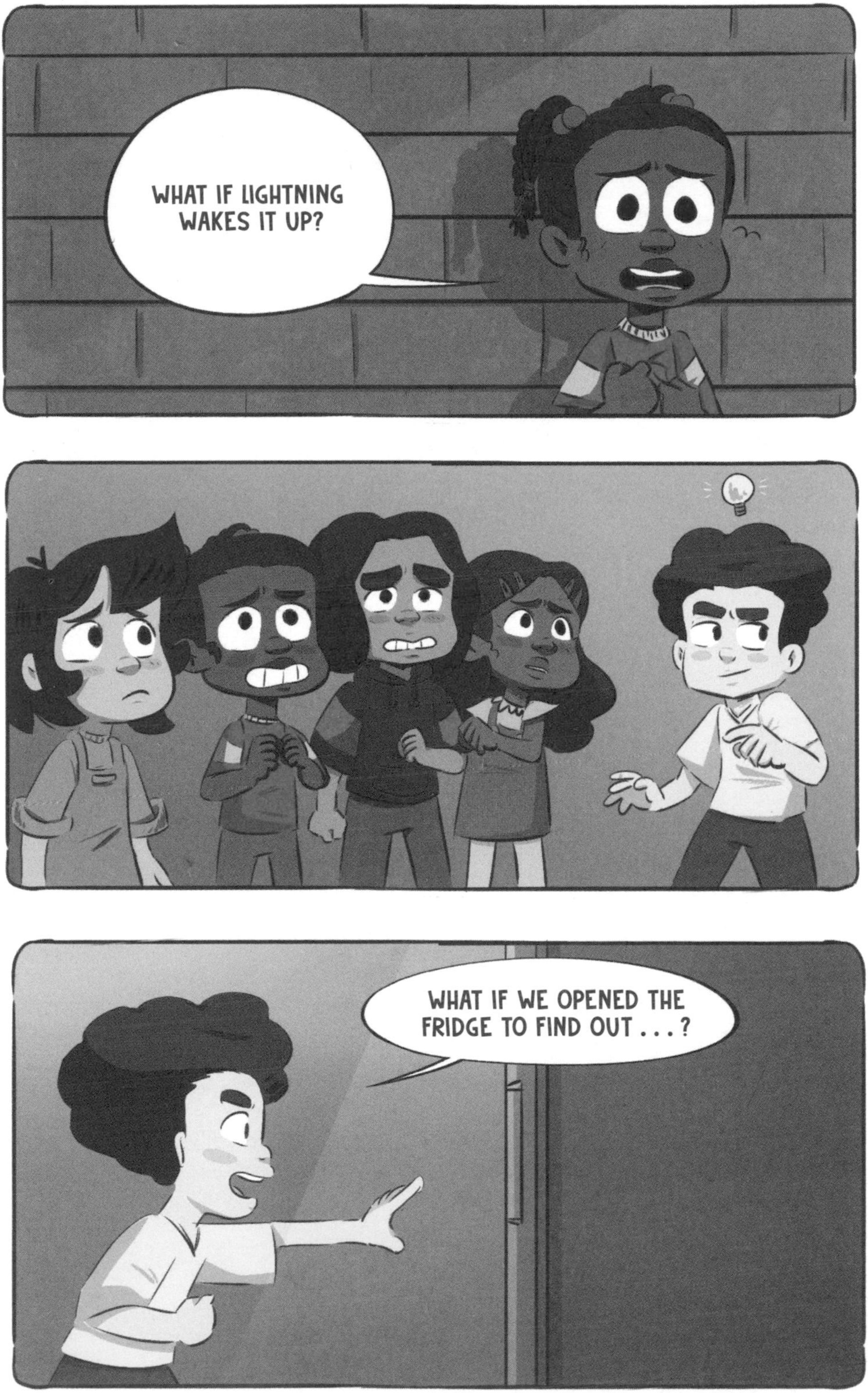
WHAT IF LIGHTNING WAKES IT UP?
WHAT IF WE OPENED THE FRIDGE TO FIND OUT . . . ?

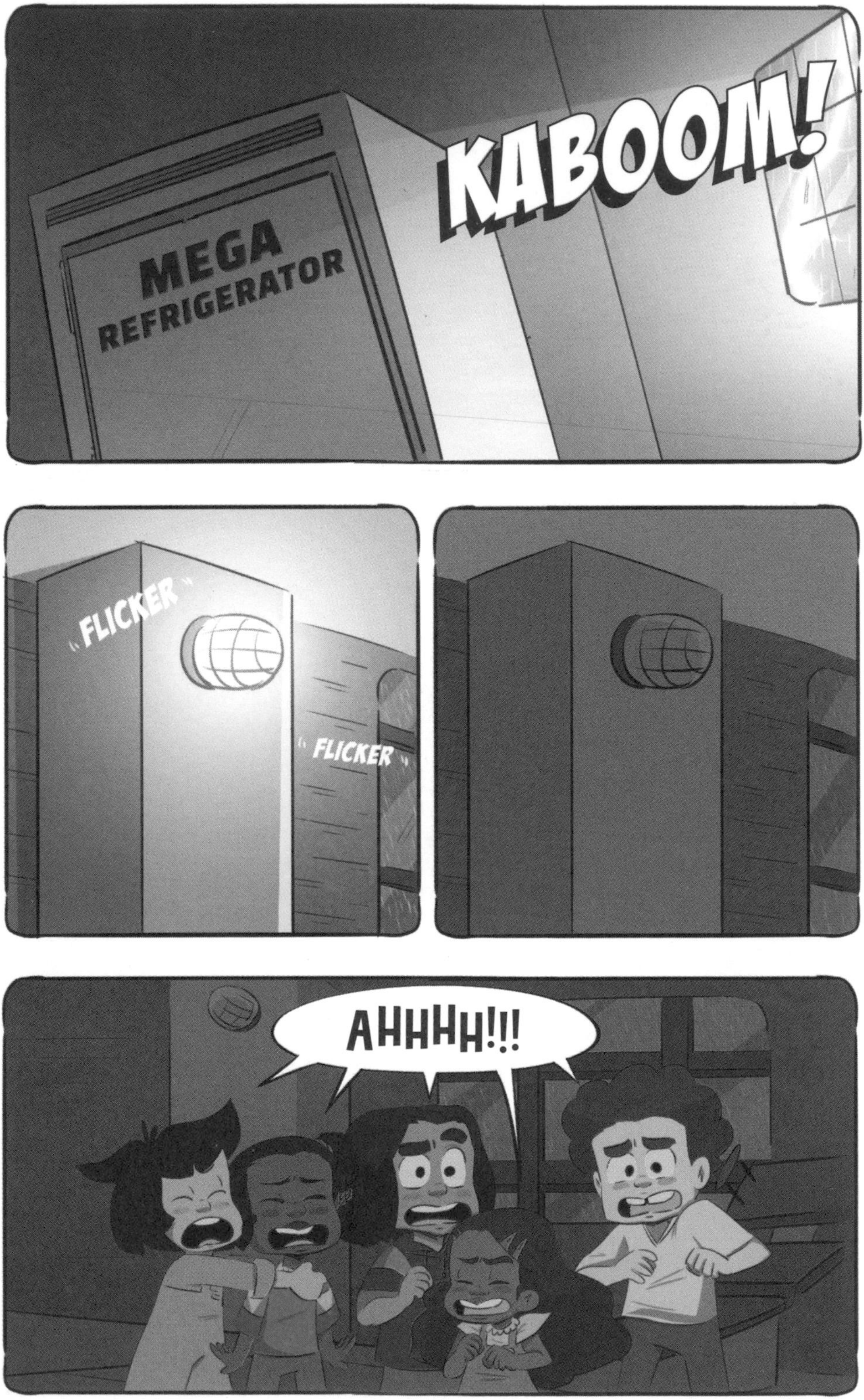
MEGA REFRIGERATOR
KABOOM!
FLICKER
FLICKER
AHHHH!!!

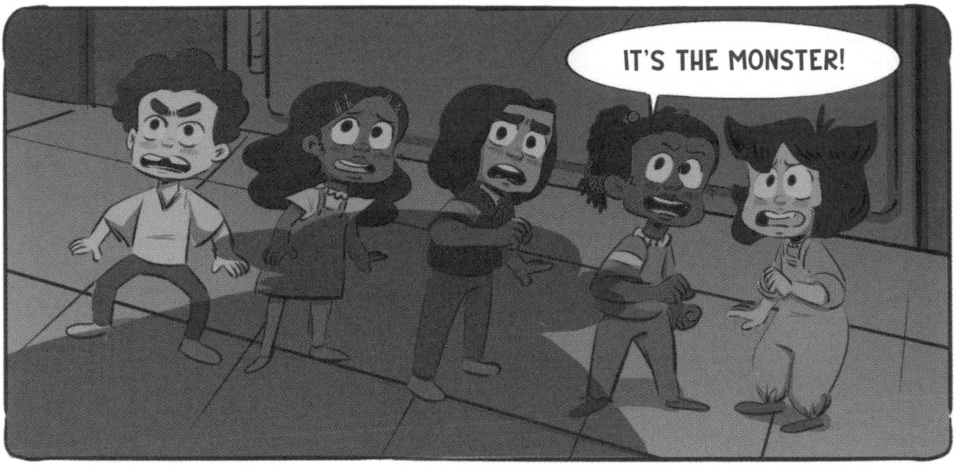
IT'S THE MONSTER!

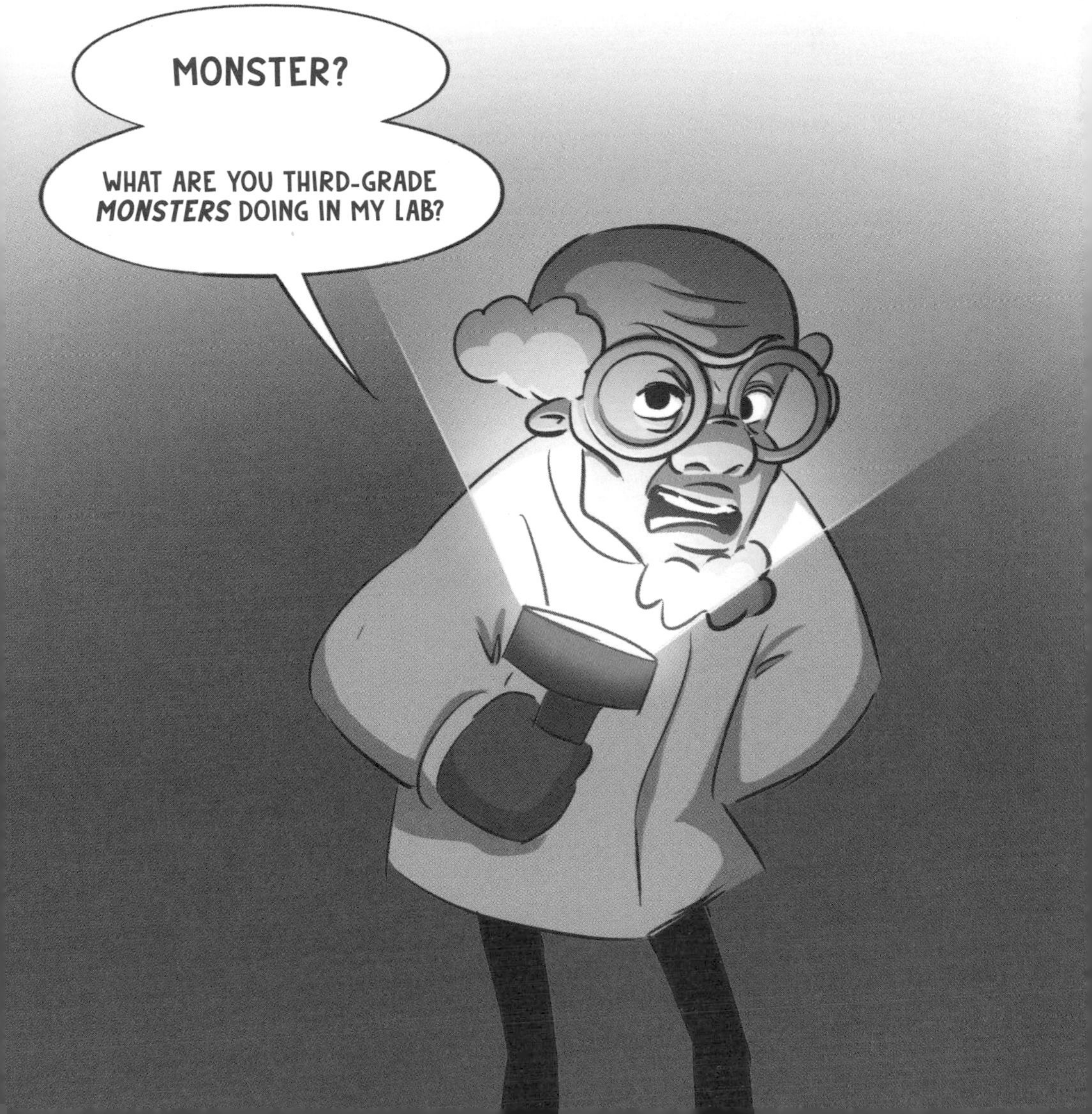
MONSTER?
WHAT ARE YOU THIRD-GRADE *MONSTERS* DOING IN MY LAB?

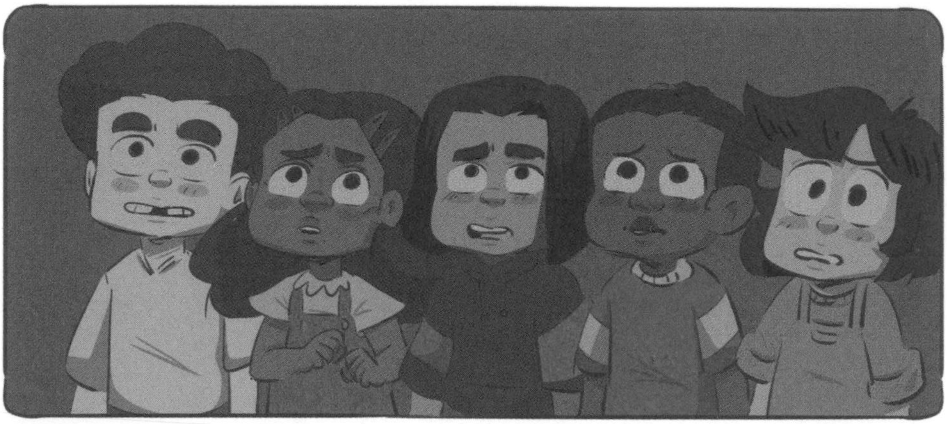

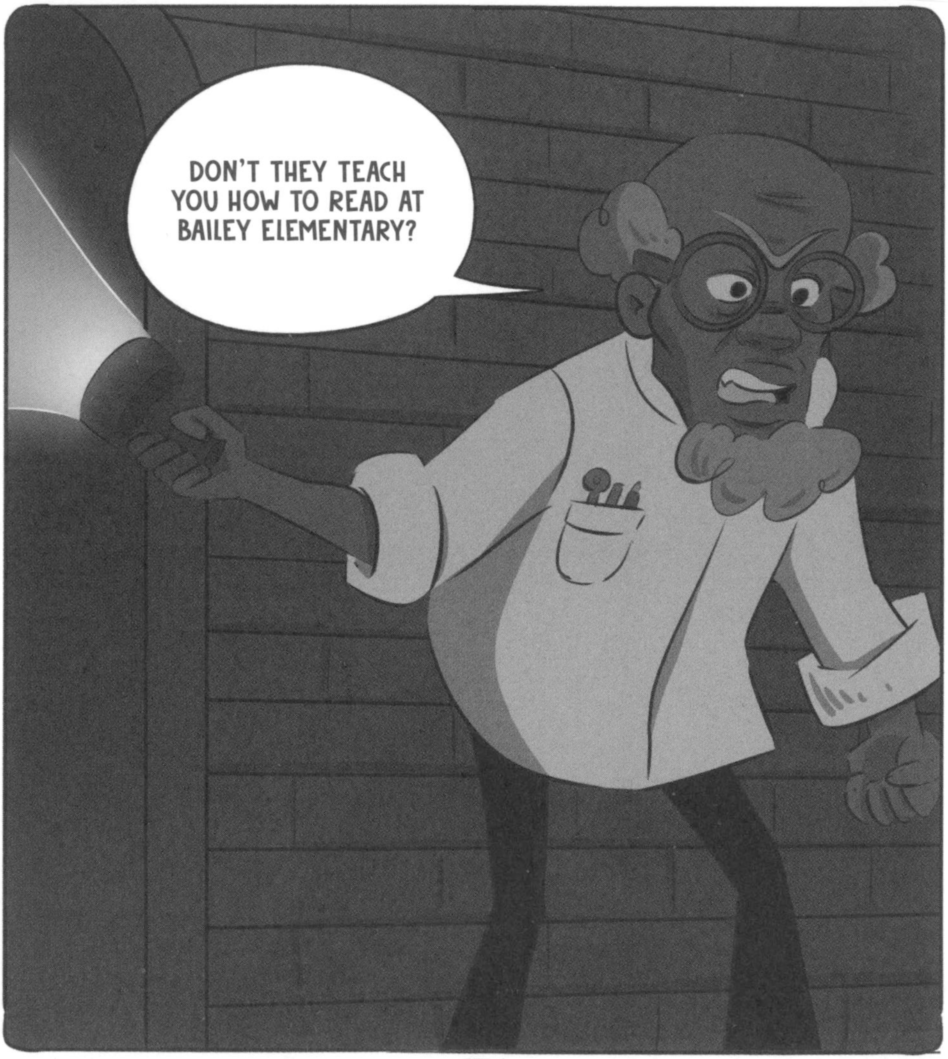
DON'T THEY TEACH YOU HOW TO READ AT BAILEY ELEMENTARY?

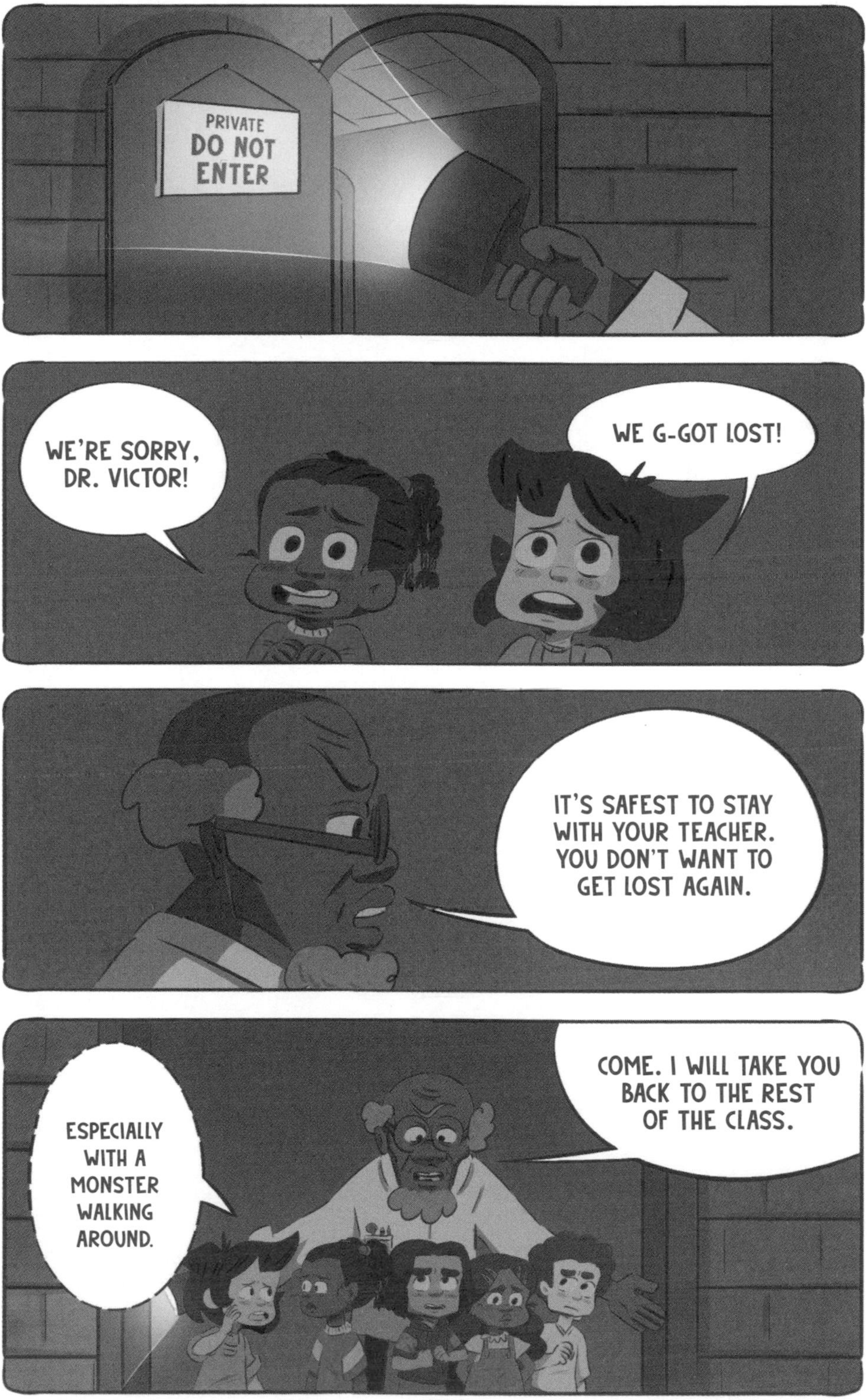
PRIVATE DO NOT ENTER
WE'RE SORRY, DR. VICTOR!
WE G-GOT LOST!
IT'S SAFEST TO STAY WITH YOUR TEACHER. YOU DON'T WANT TO GET LOST AGAIN.
ESPECIALLY WITH A MONSTER WALKING AROUND.
COME. I WILL TAKE YOU BACK TO THE REST OF THE CLASS.

CHAPTER 4 THE STORM

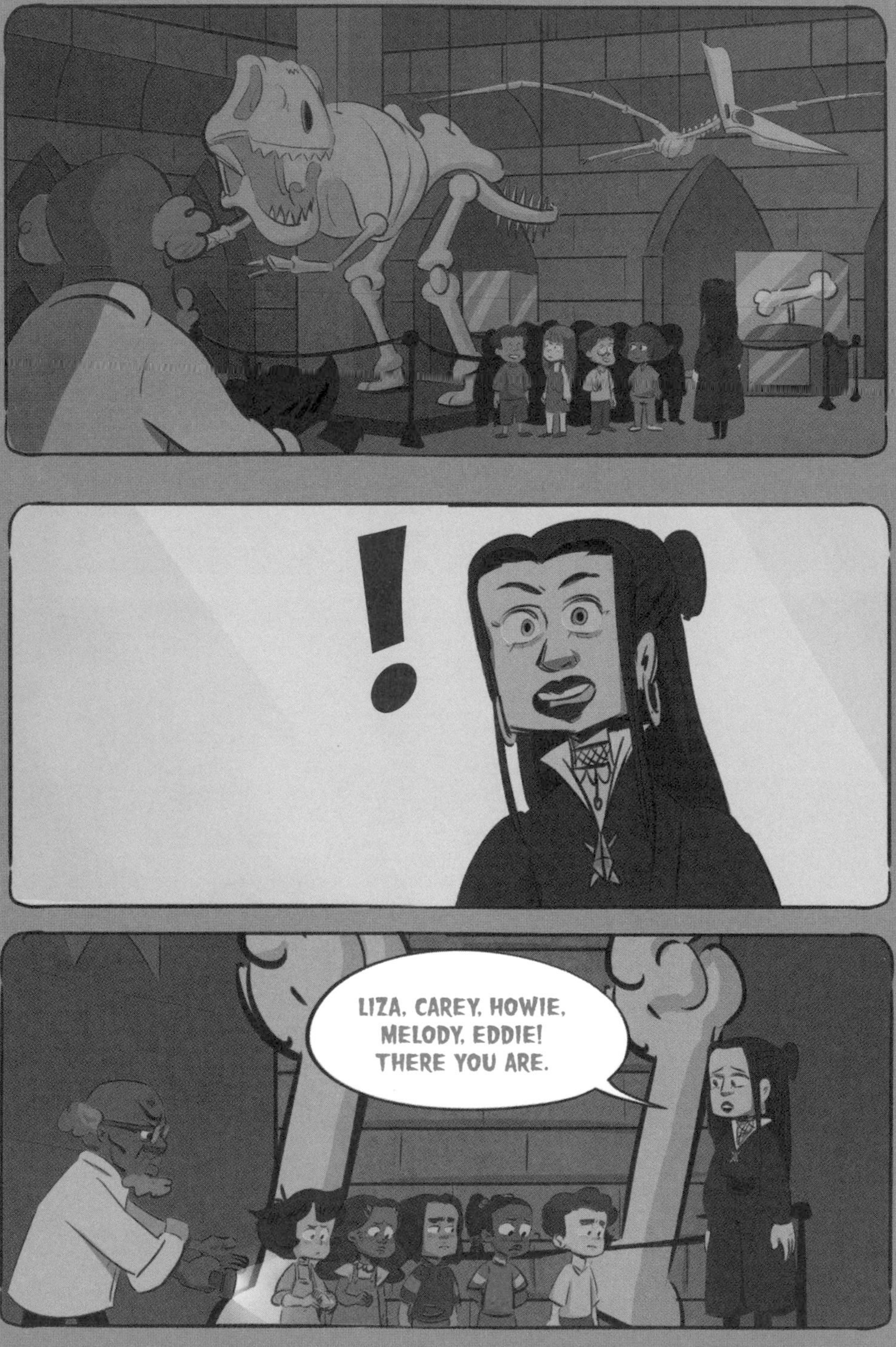
!
LIZA, CAREY, HOWIE, MELODY, EDDIE! THERE YOU ARE.

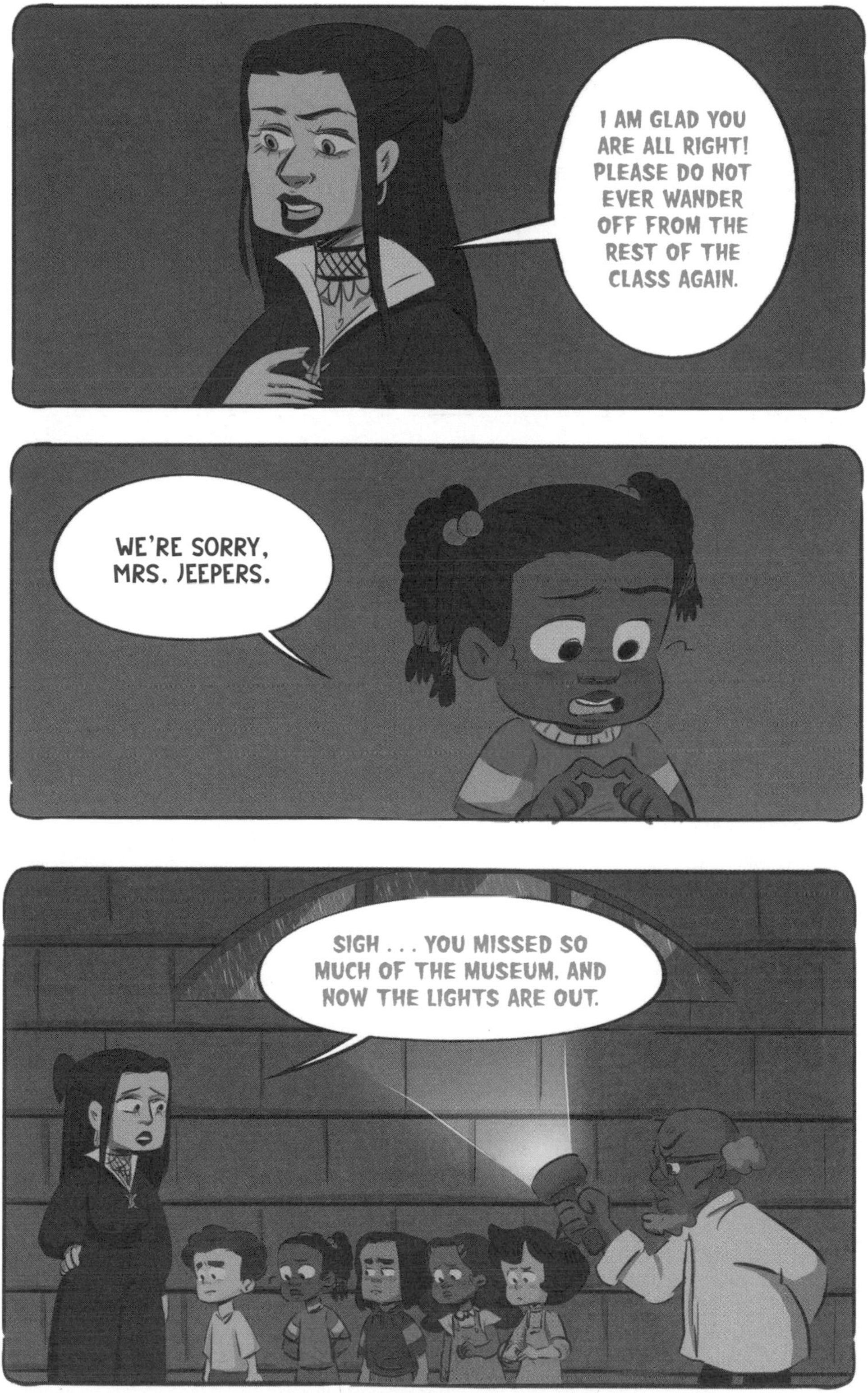
I AM GLAD YOU ARE ALL RIGHT! PLEASE DO NOT EVER WANDER OFF FROM THE REST OF THE CLASS AGAIN.
WE'RE SORRY, MRS. JEEPERS.
SIGH . . . YOU MISSED SO MUCH OF THE MUSEUM, AND NOW THE LIGHTS ARE OUT.

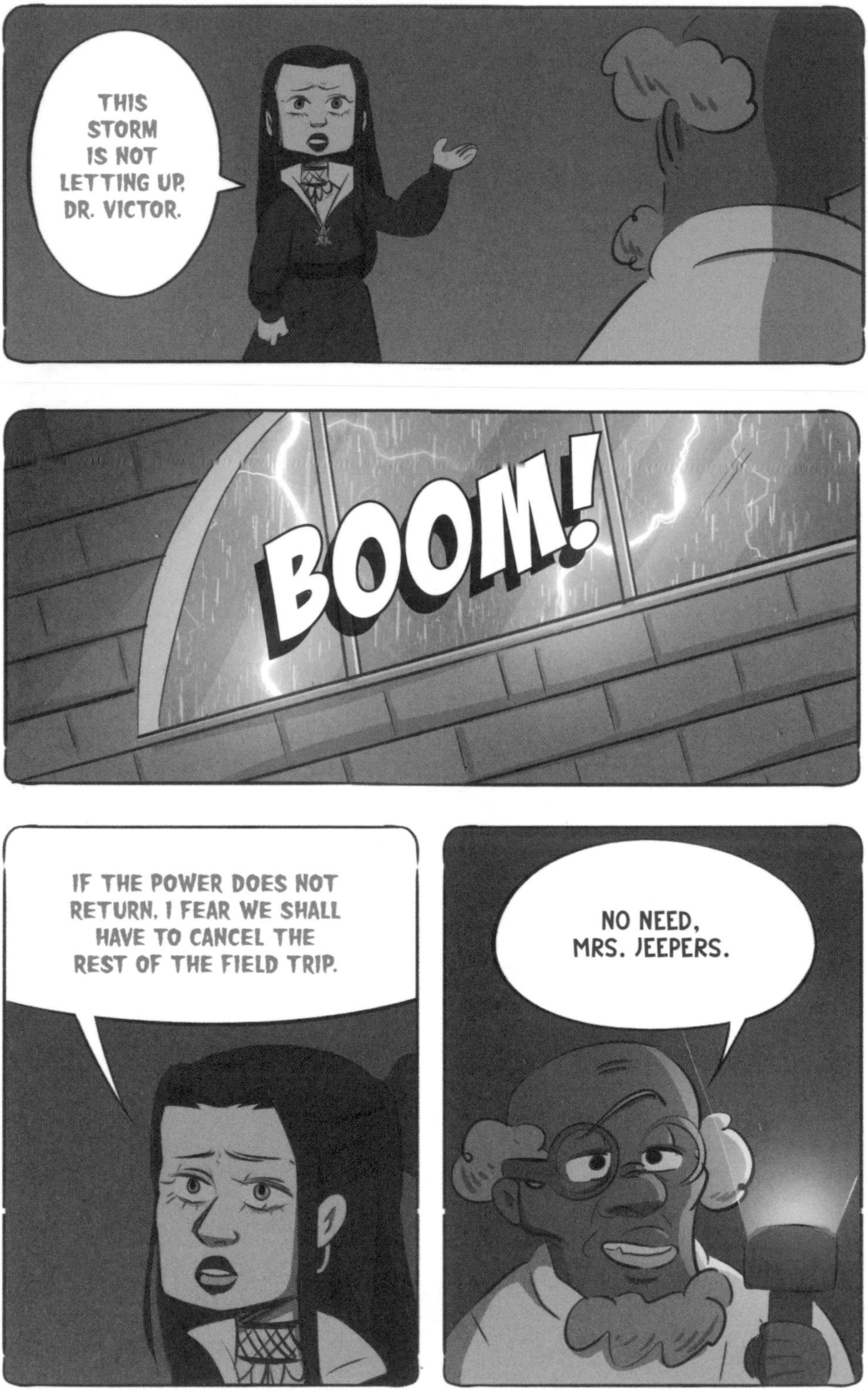
THIS STORM IS NOT LETTING UP, DR. VICTOR.
BOOM!
IF THE POWER DOES NOT RETURN, I FEAR WE SHALL HAVE TO CANCEL THE REST OF THE FIELD TRIP.
NO NEED, MRS. JEEPERS.

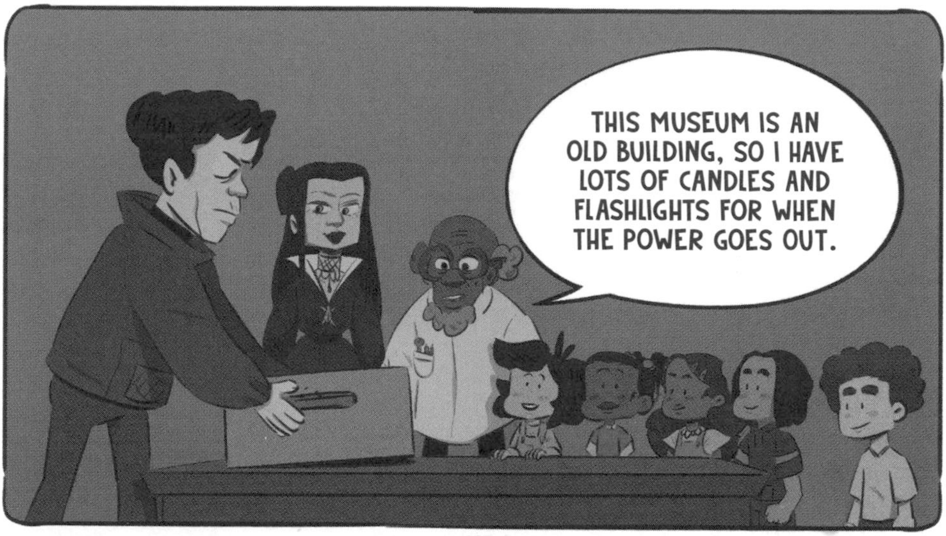
THIS MUSEUM IS AN OLD BUILDING, SO I HAVE LOTS OF CANDLES AND FLASHLIGHTS FOR WHEN THE POWER GOES OUT.

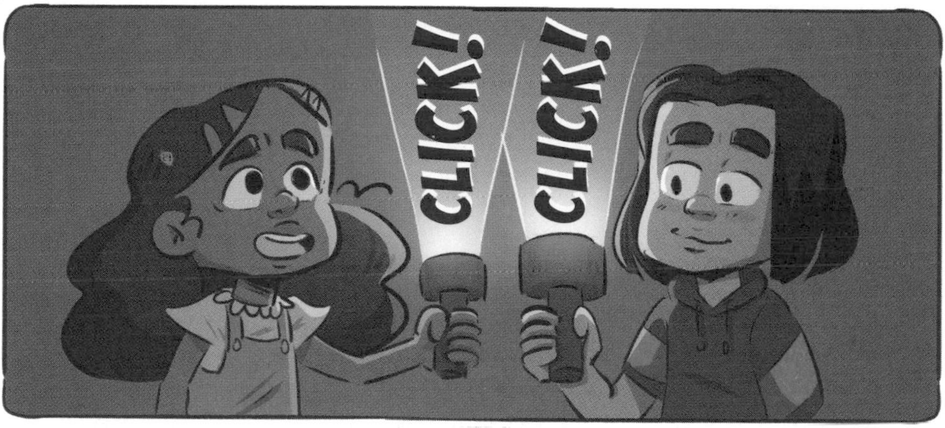
CLICK!
CLICK!

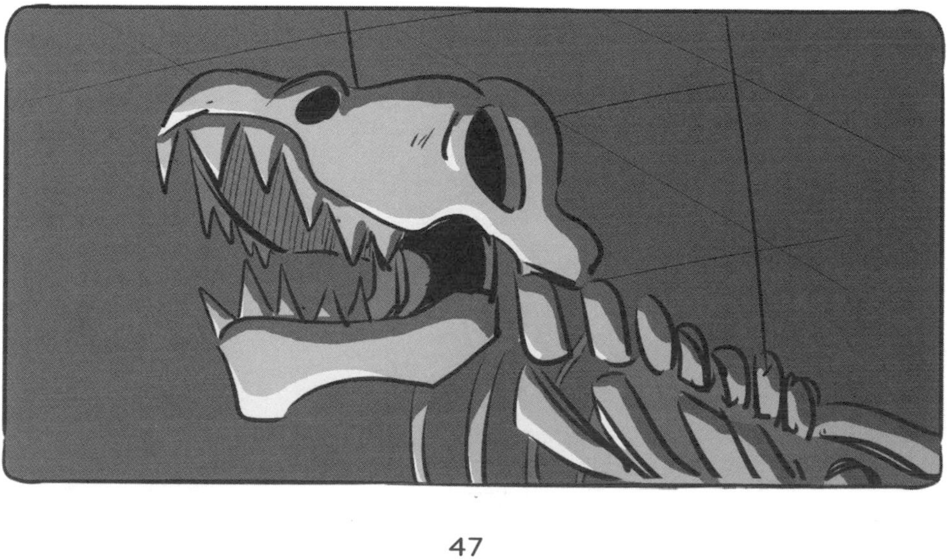

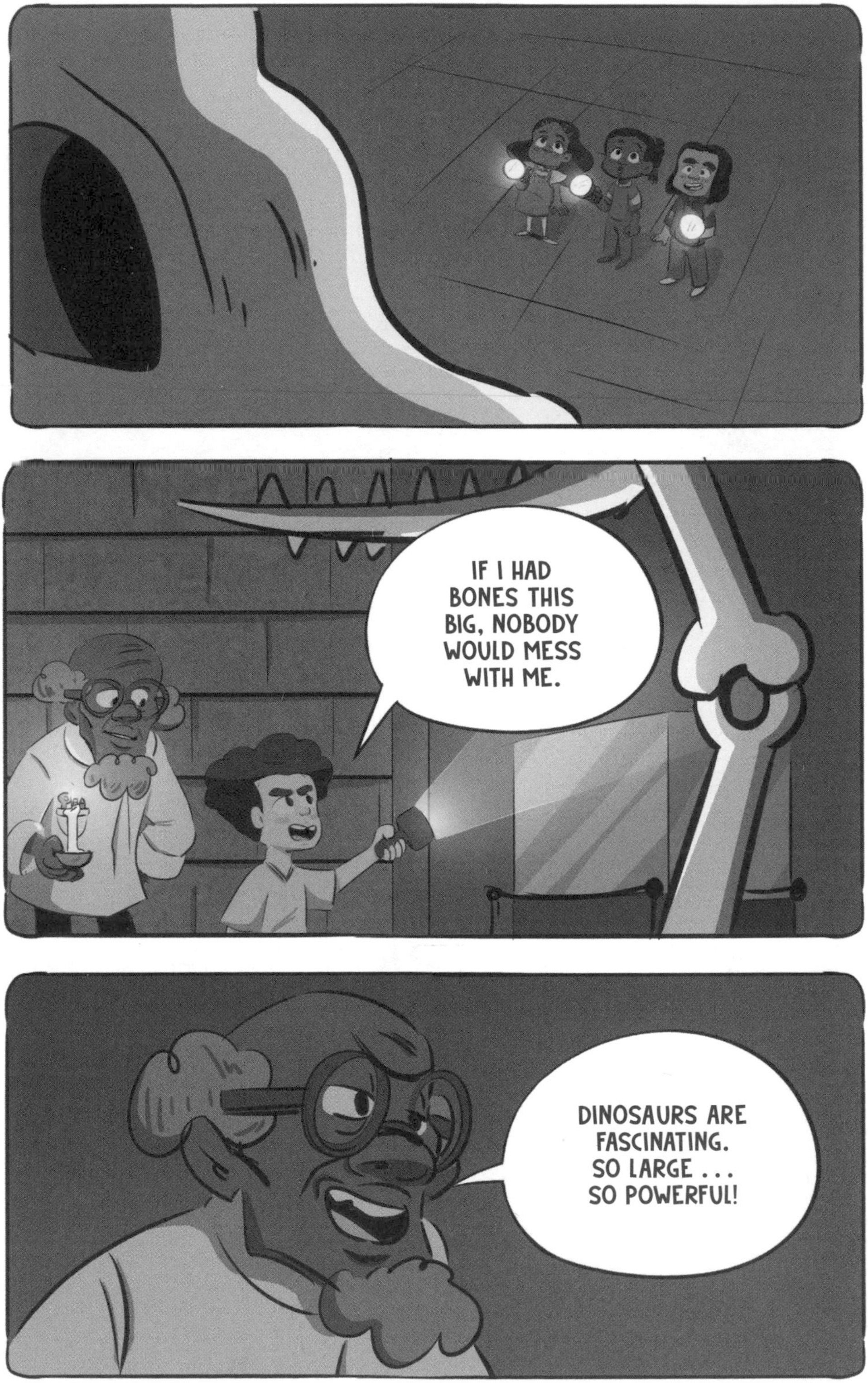
IF I HAD BONES THIS BIG, NOBODY WOULD MESS WITH ME.
DINOSAURS ARE FASCINATING. SO LARGE . . . SO POWERFUL!

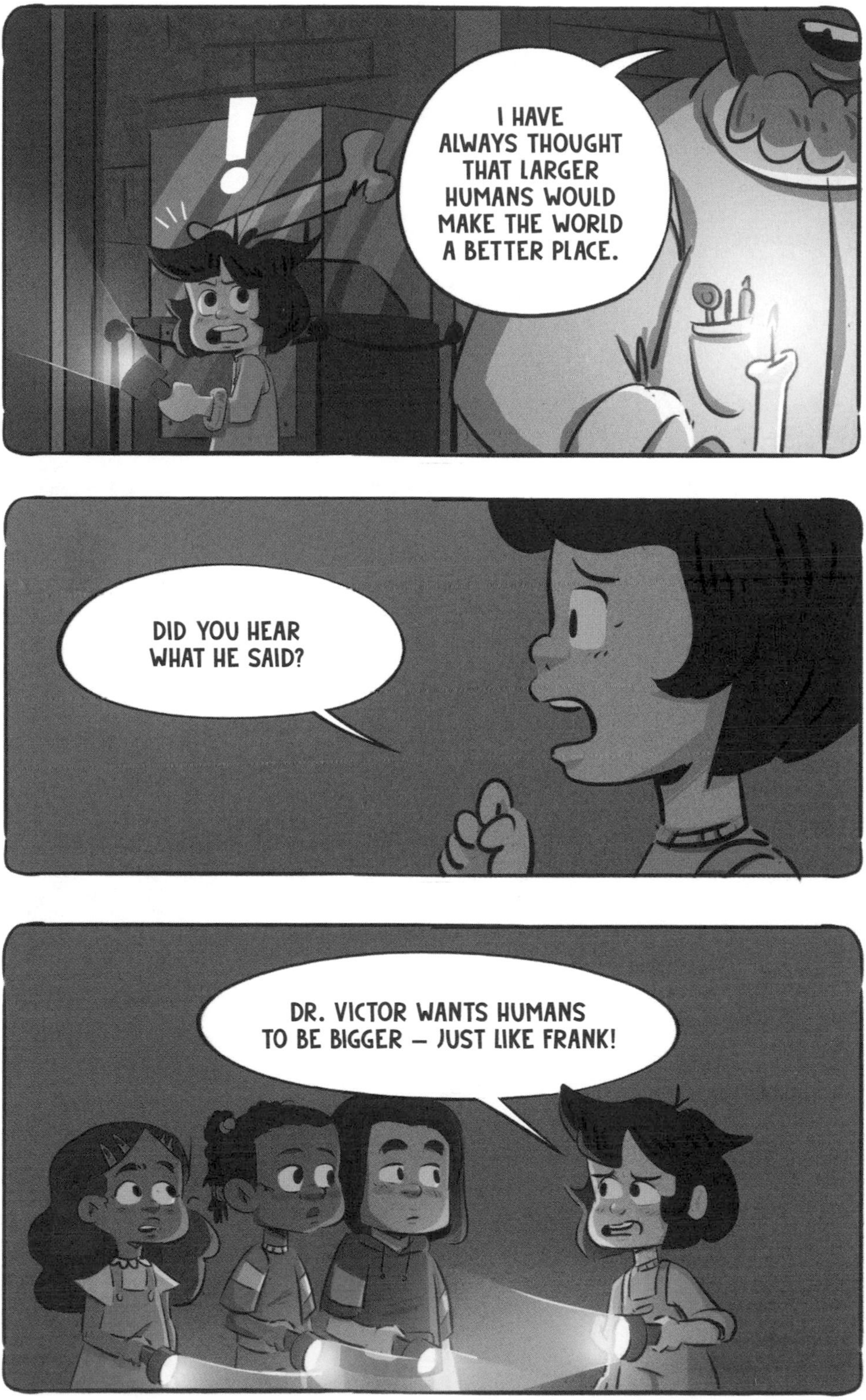
!
I HAVE ALWAYS THOUGHT THAT LARGER HUMANS WOULD MAKE THE WORLD A BETTER PLACE.
DID YOU HEAR WHAT HE SAID?
DR. VICTOR WANTS HUMANS TO BE BIGGER — JUST LIKE FRANK!

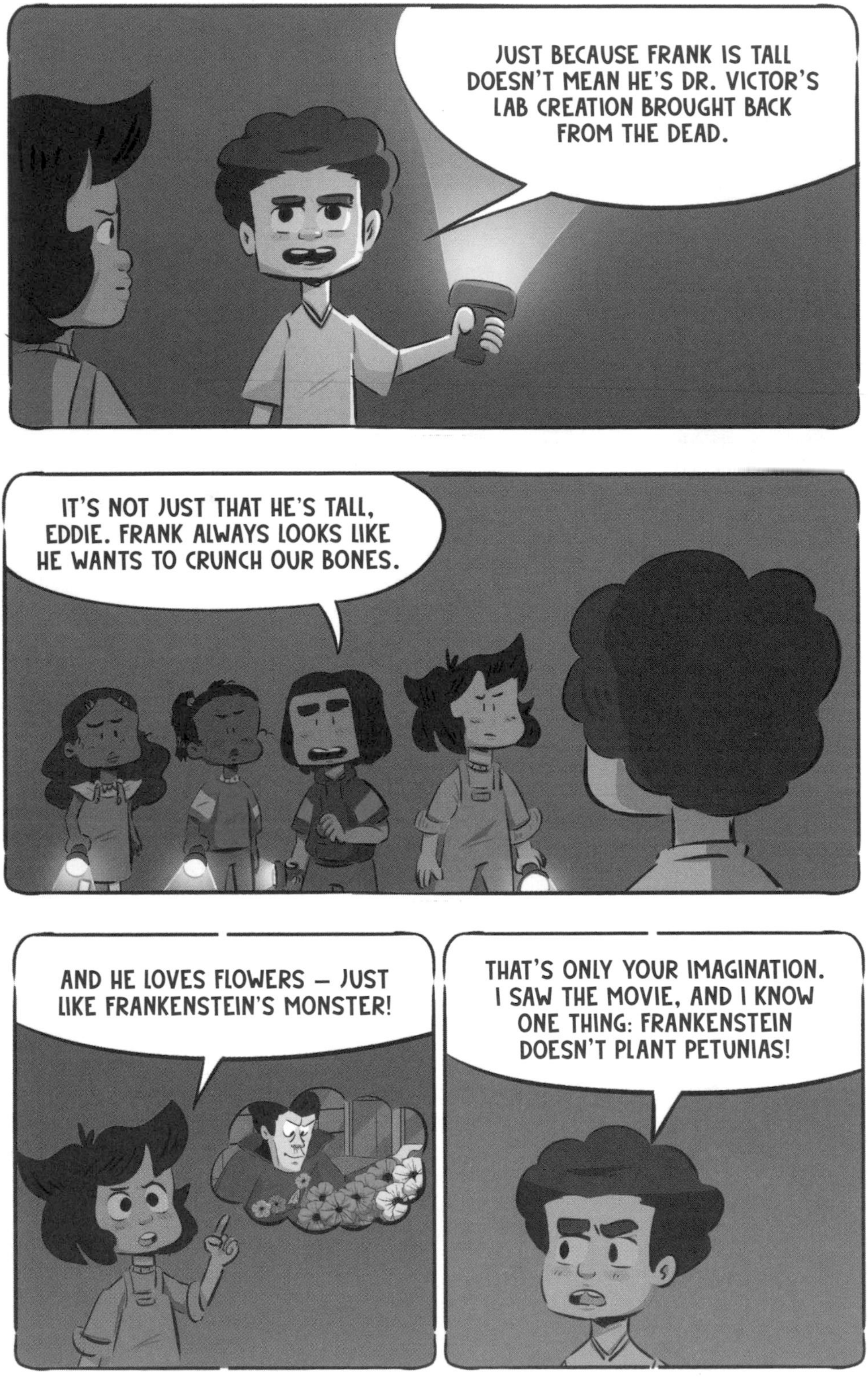
JUST BECAUSE FRANK IS TALL DOESN'T MEAN HE'S DR. VICTOR'S LAB CREATION BROUGHT BACK FROM THE DEAD.
IT'S NOT JUST THAT HE'S TALL, EDDIE. FRANK ALWAYS LOOKS LIKE HE WANTS TO CRUNCH OUR BONES.
AND HE LOVES FLOWERS – JUST LIKE FRANKENSTEIN'S MONSTER!
THAT'S ONLY YOUR IMAGINATION. I SAW THE MOVIE, AND I KNOW ONE THING: FRANKENSTEIN DOESN'T PLANT PETUNIAS!

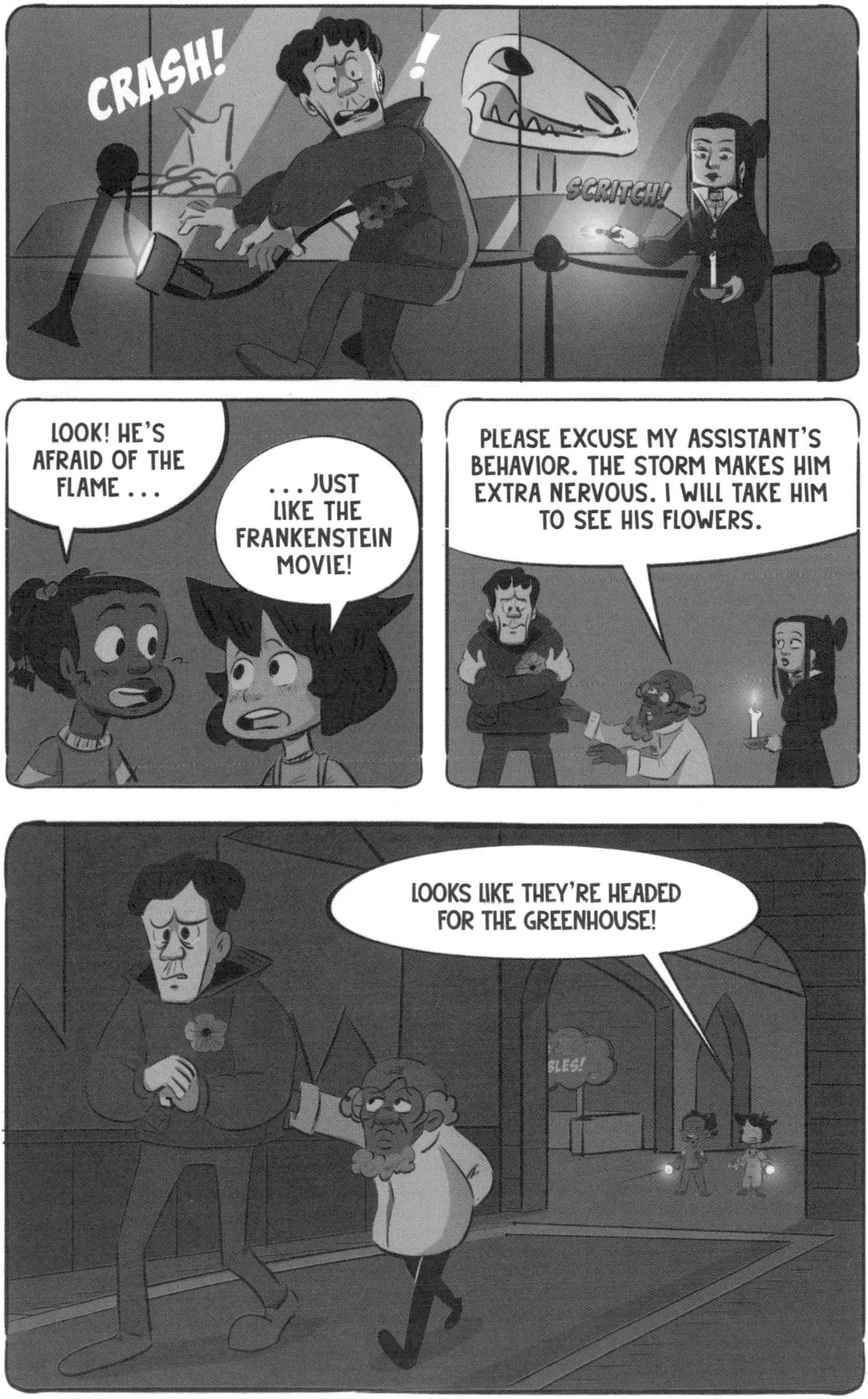
CRASH!
SCRITCH!
LOOK! HE'S AFRAID OF THE FLAME . . .
. . . JUST LIKE THE FRANKENSTEIN MOVIE!
PLEASE EXCUSE MY ASSISTANT'S BEHAVIOR. THE STORM MAKES HIM EXTRA NERVOUS. I WILL TAKE HIM TO SEE HIS FLOWERS.
LOOKS LIKE THEY'RE HEADED FOR THE GREENHOUSE!

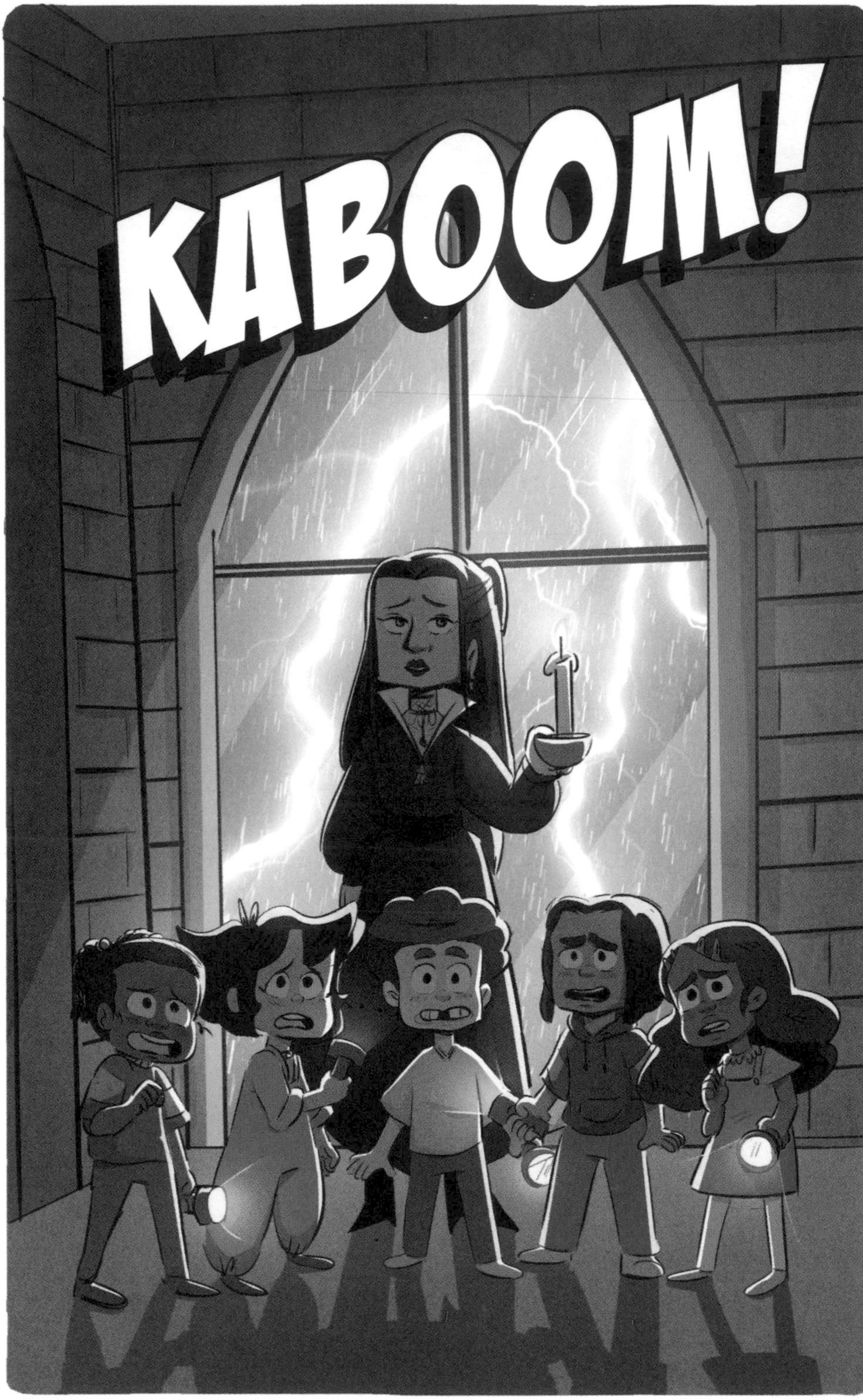
KABOOM!

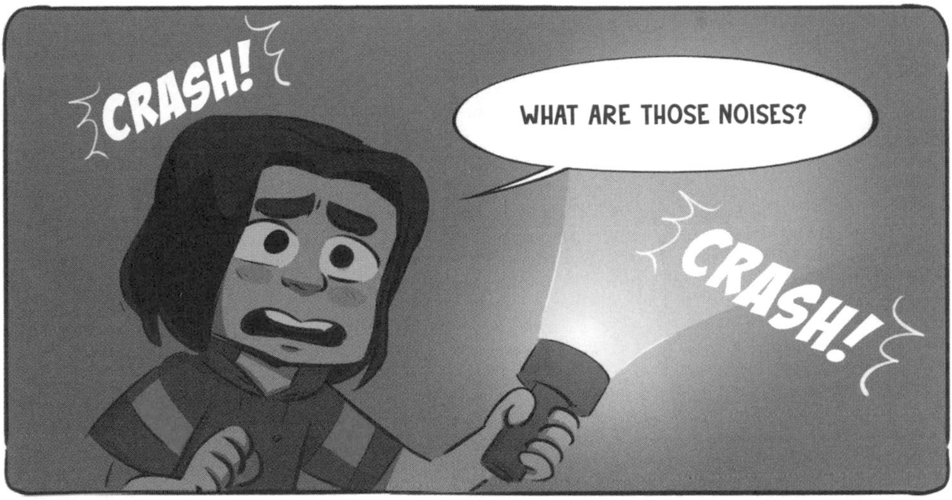
CRASH!
WHAT ARE THOSE NOISES?
CRASH!

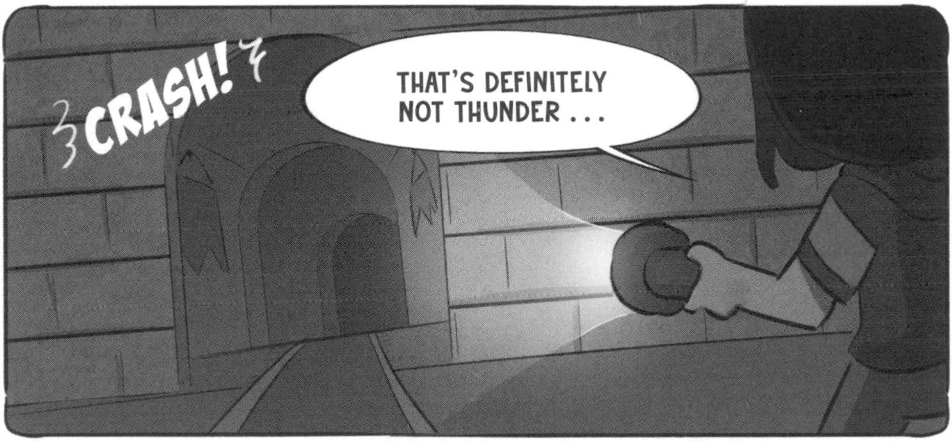
CRASH!
THAT'S DEFINITELY NOT THUNDER . . .

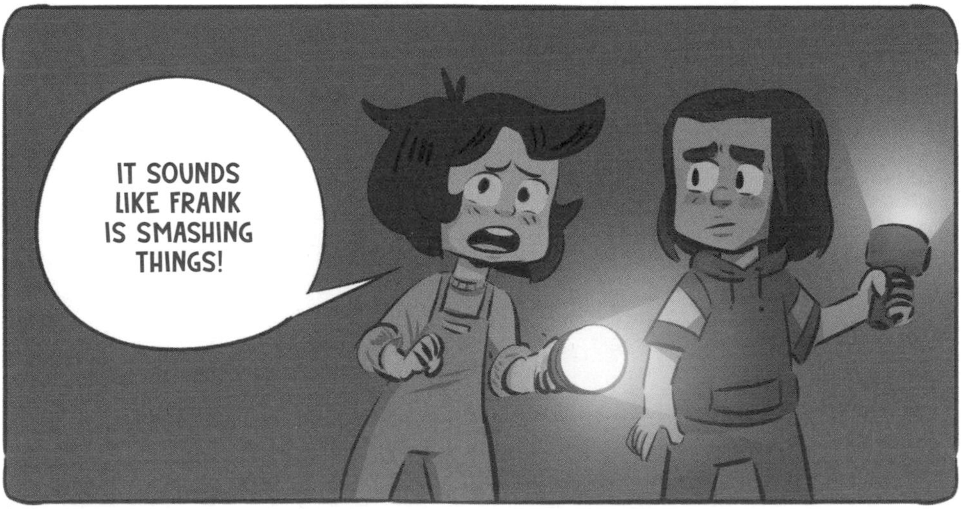
IT SOUNDS LIKE FRANK IS SMASHING THINGS!

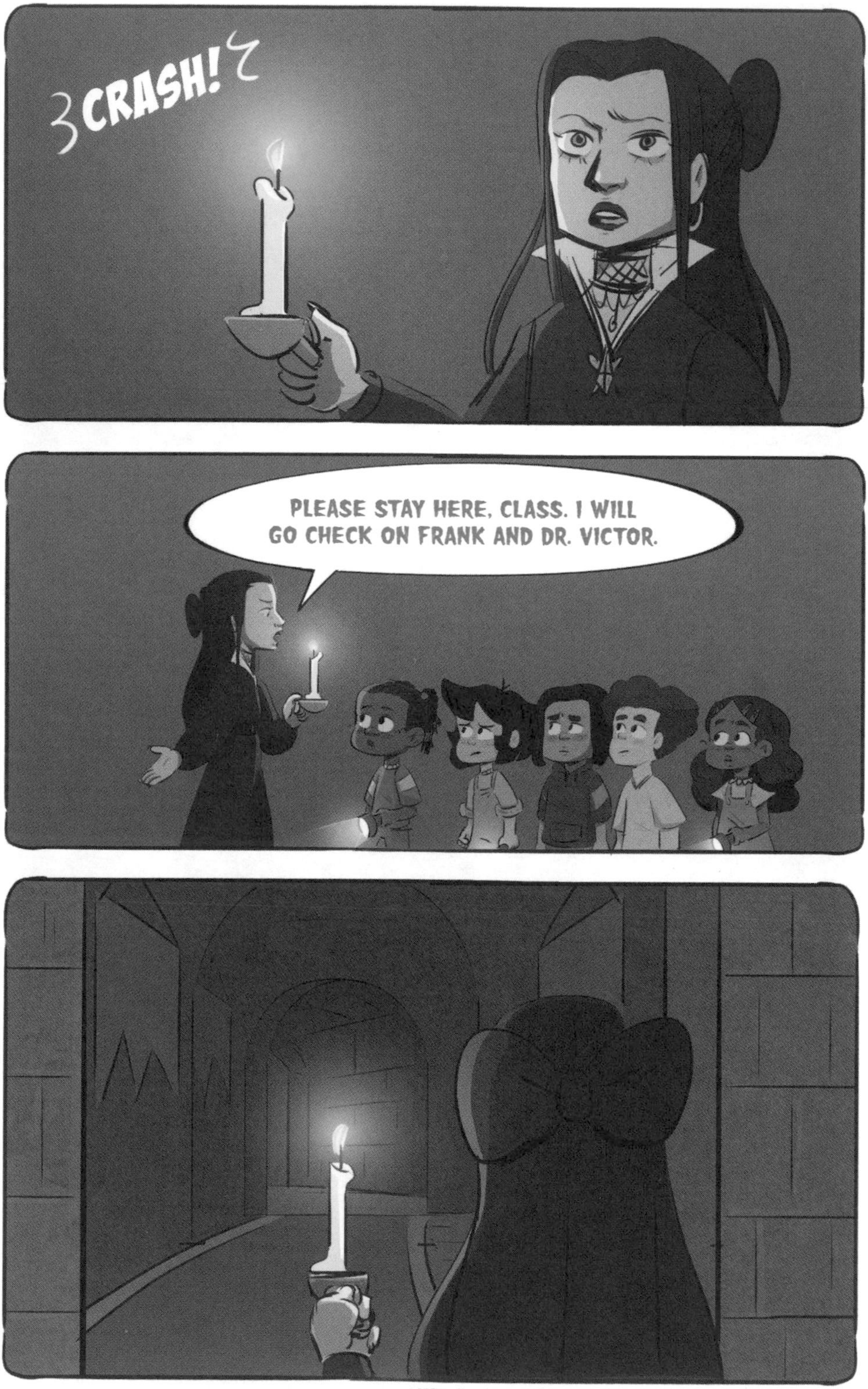
CRASH!
PLEASE STAY HERE, CLASS. I WILL GO CHECK ON FRANK AND DR. VICTOR.

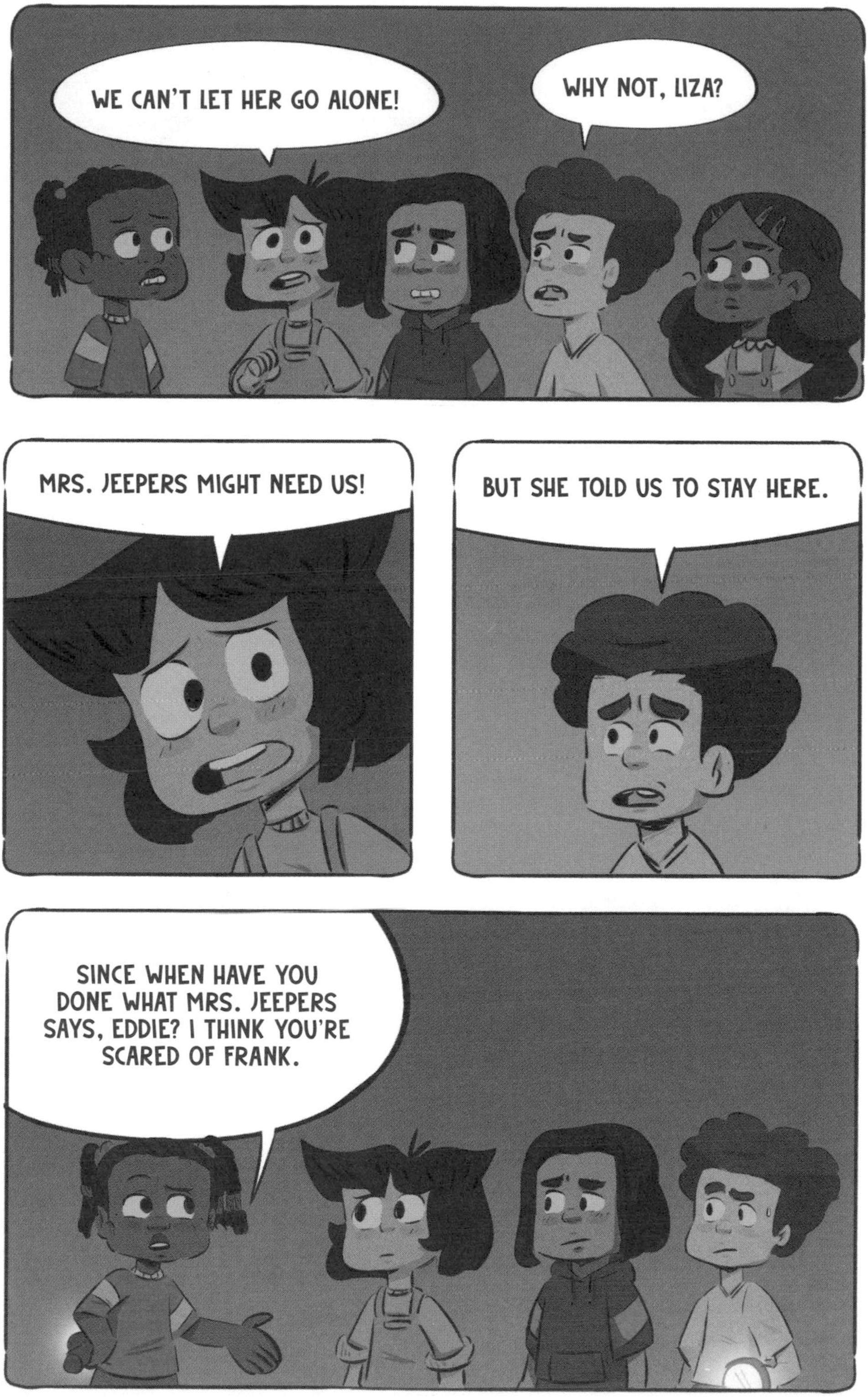
WE CAN'T LET HER GO ALONE!
WHY NOT, LIZA?
MRS. JEEPERS MIGHT NEED US!
BUT SHE TOLD US TO STAY HERE.
SINCE WHEN HAVE YOU DONE WHAT MRS. JEEPERS SAYS, EDDIE? I THINK YOU'RE SCARED OF FRANK.

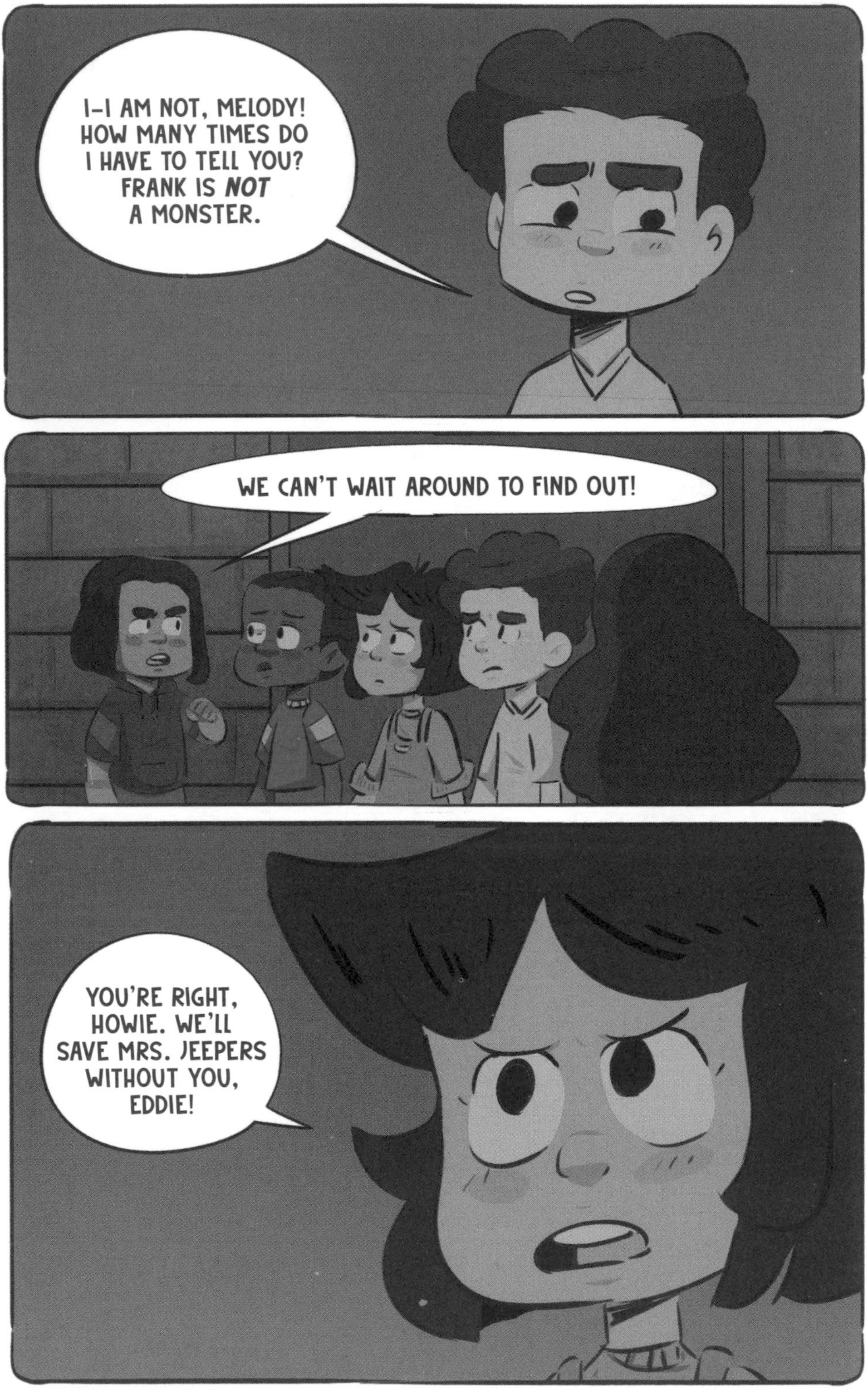
I-I AM NOT, MELODY! HOW MANY TIMES DO I HAVE TO TELL YOU? FRANK IS ***NOT*** A MONSTER.
WE CAN'T WAIT AROUND TO FIND OUT!
YOU'RE RIGHT, HOWIE. WE'LL SAVE MRS. JEEPERS WITHOUT YOU, EDDIE!

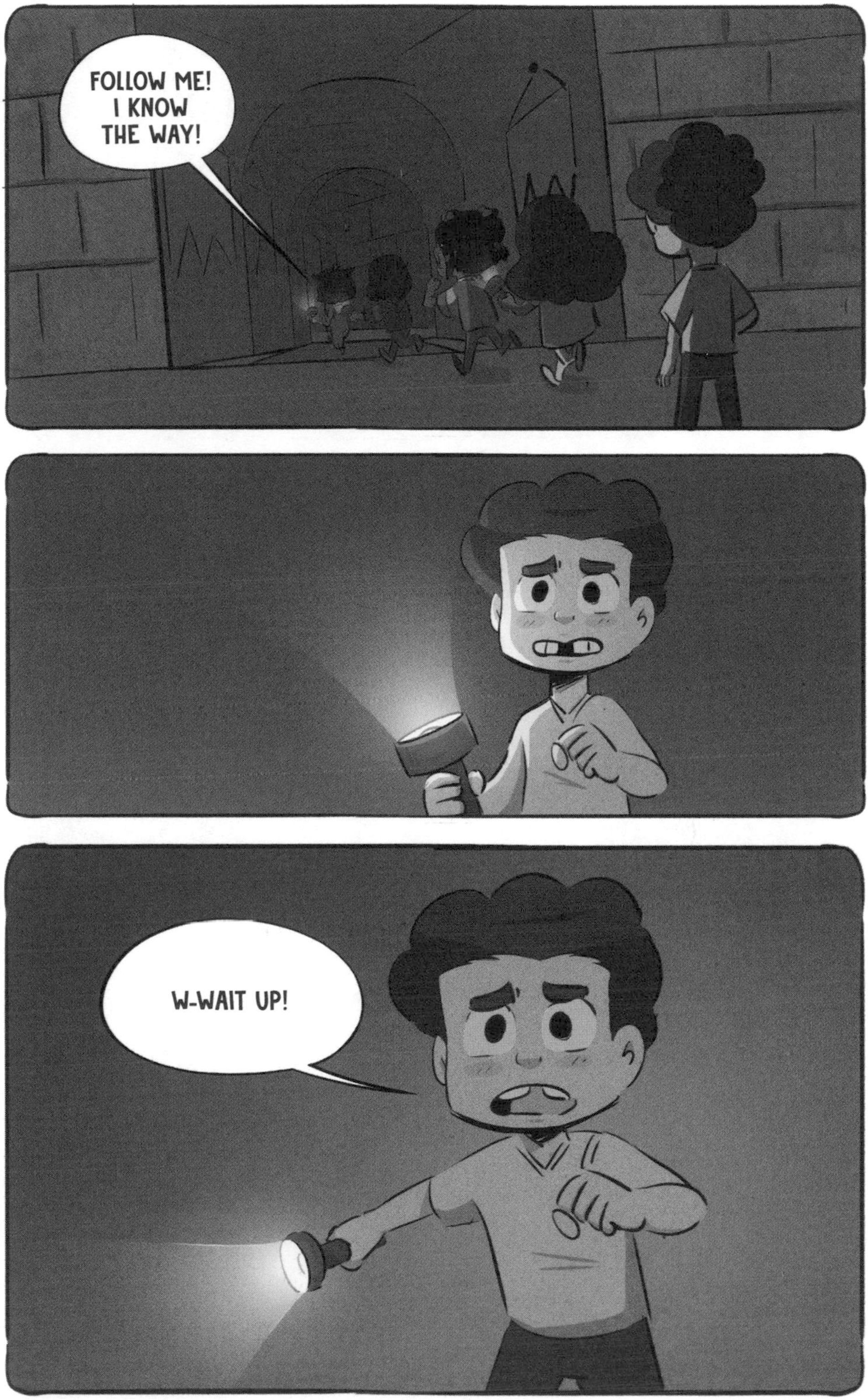
FOLLOW ME! I KNOW THE WAY!
W-WAIT UP!

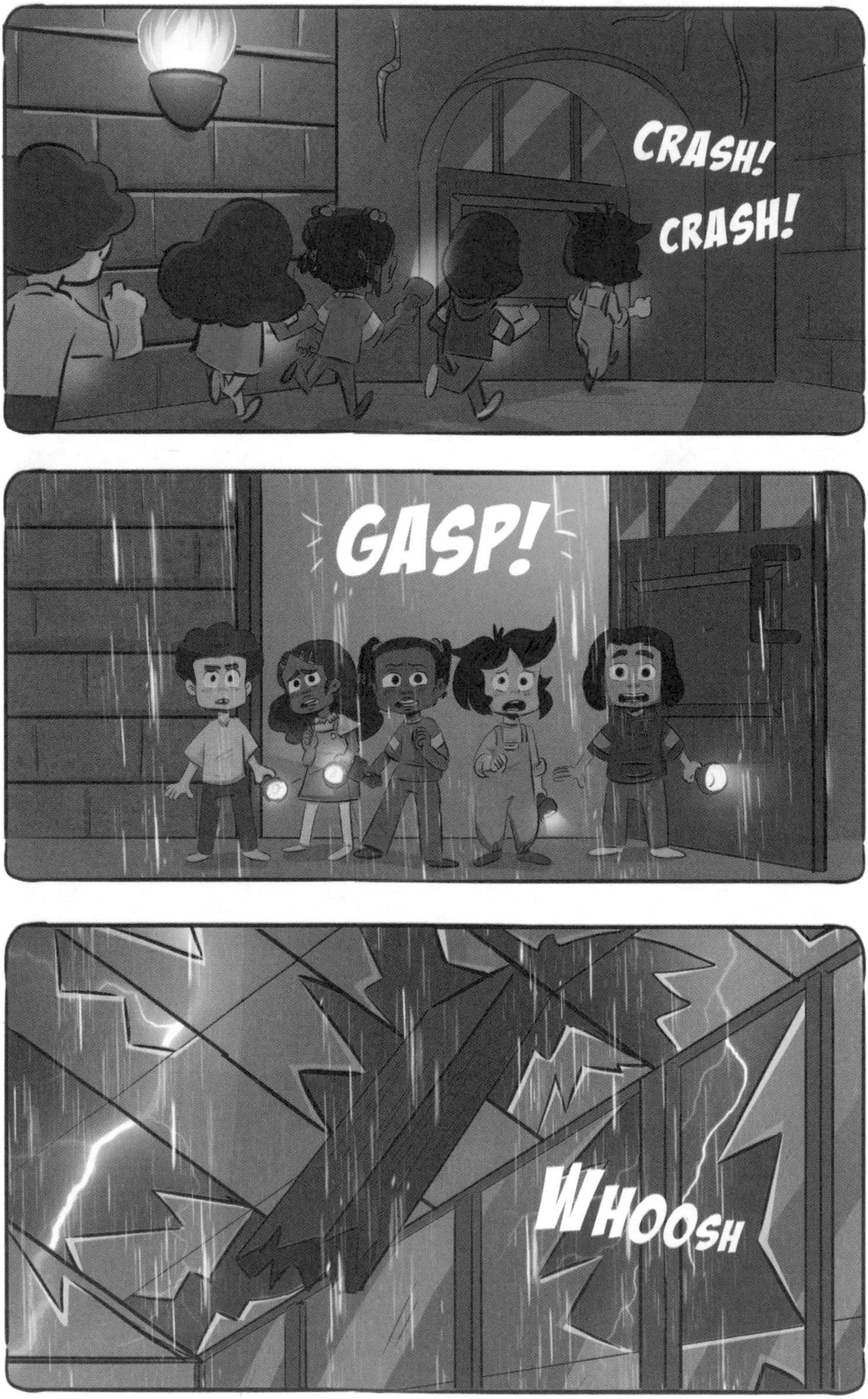
CRASH!
CRASH!
GASP!
WHOOSH

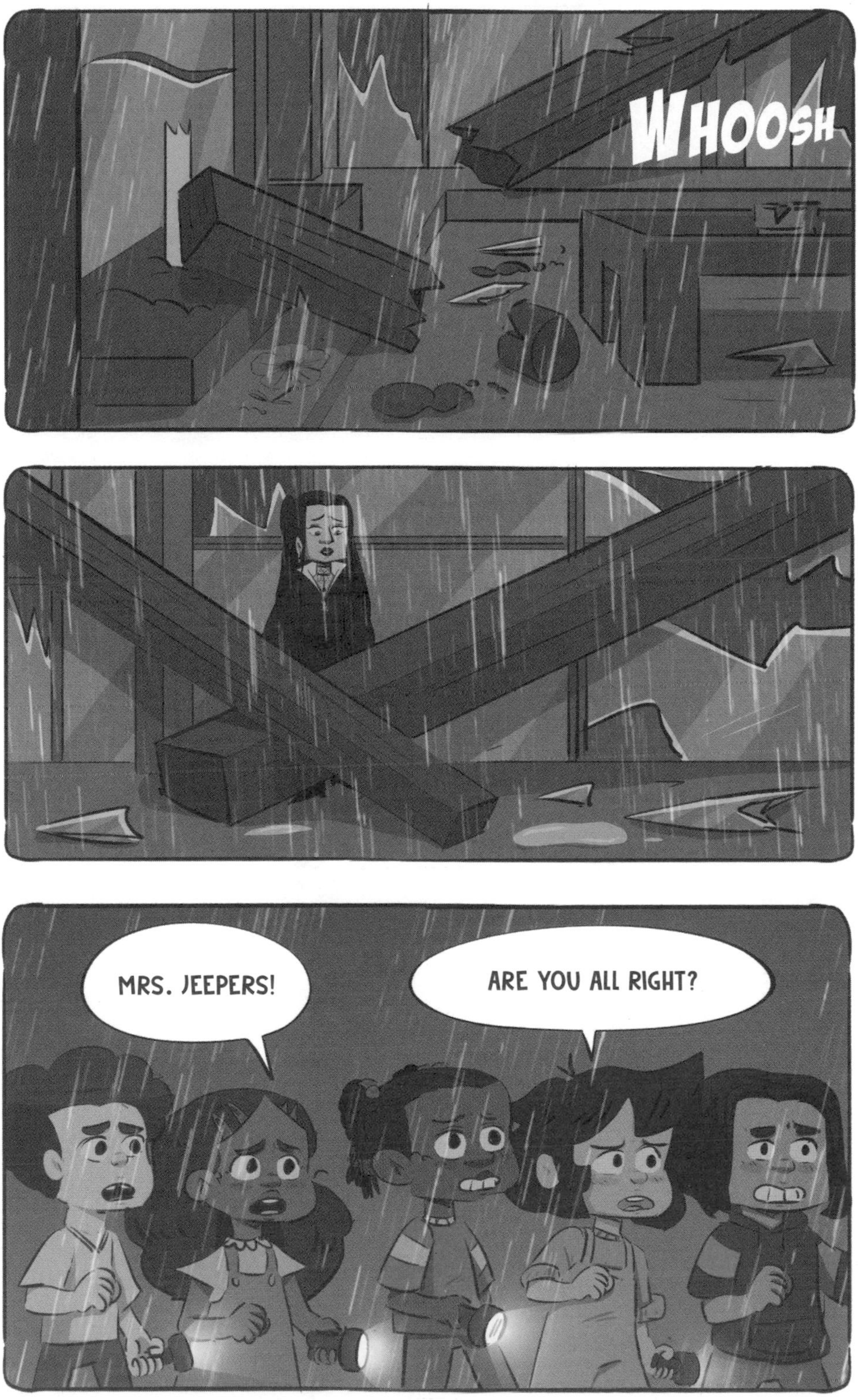
WHOOSH
MRS. JEEPERS!
ARE YOU ALL RIGHT?

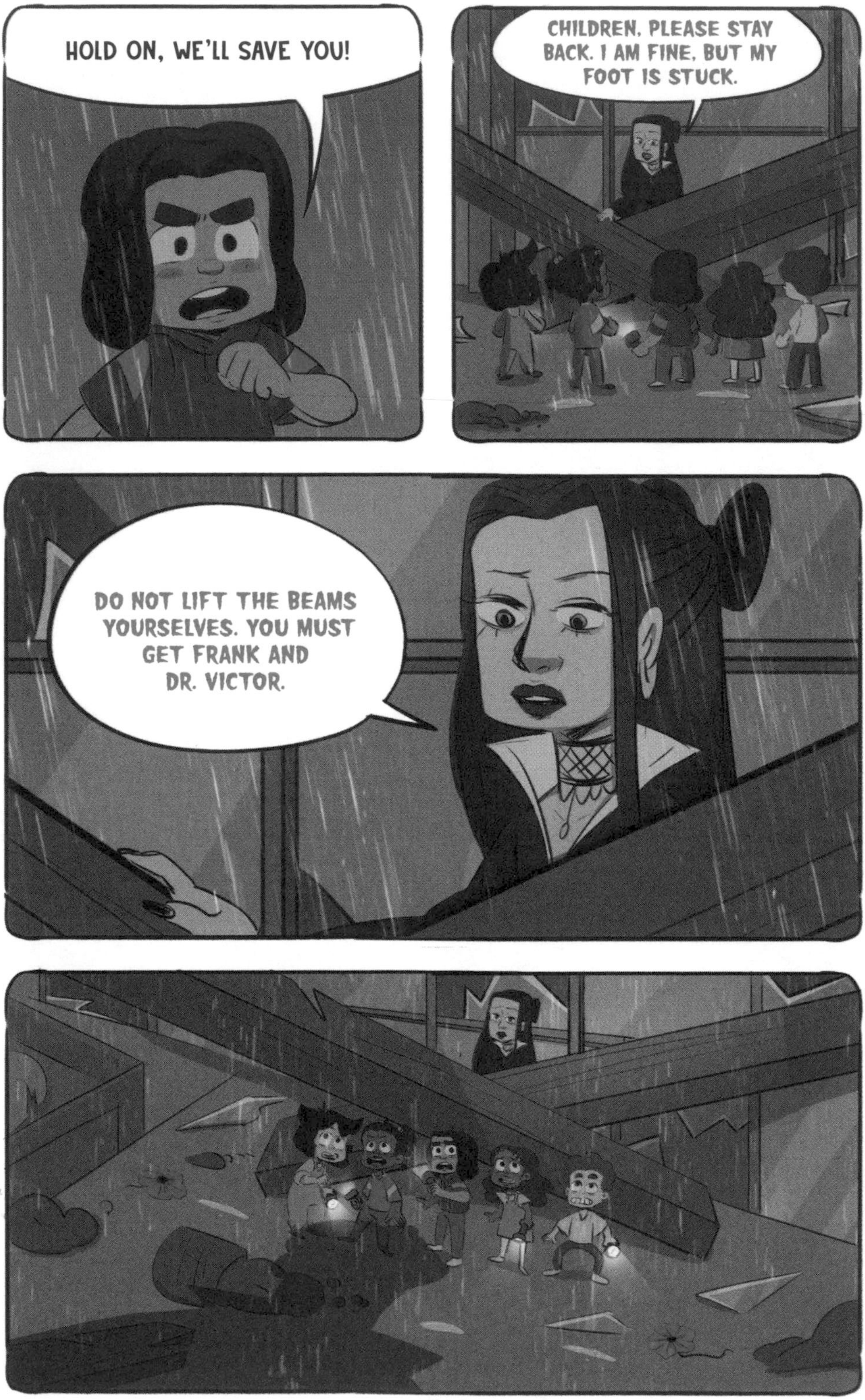
HOLD ON, WE'LL SAVE YOU!
CHILDREN, PLEASE STAY BACK. I AM FINE, BUT MY FOOT IS STUCK.
DO NOT LIFT THE BEAMS YOURSELVES. YOU MUST GET FRANK AND DR. VICTOR.

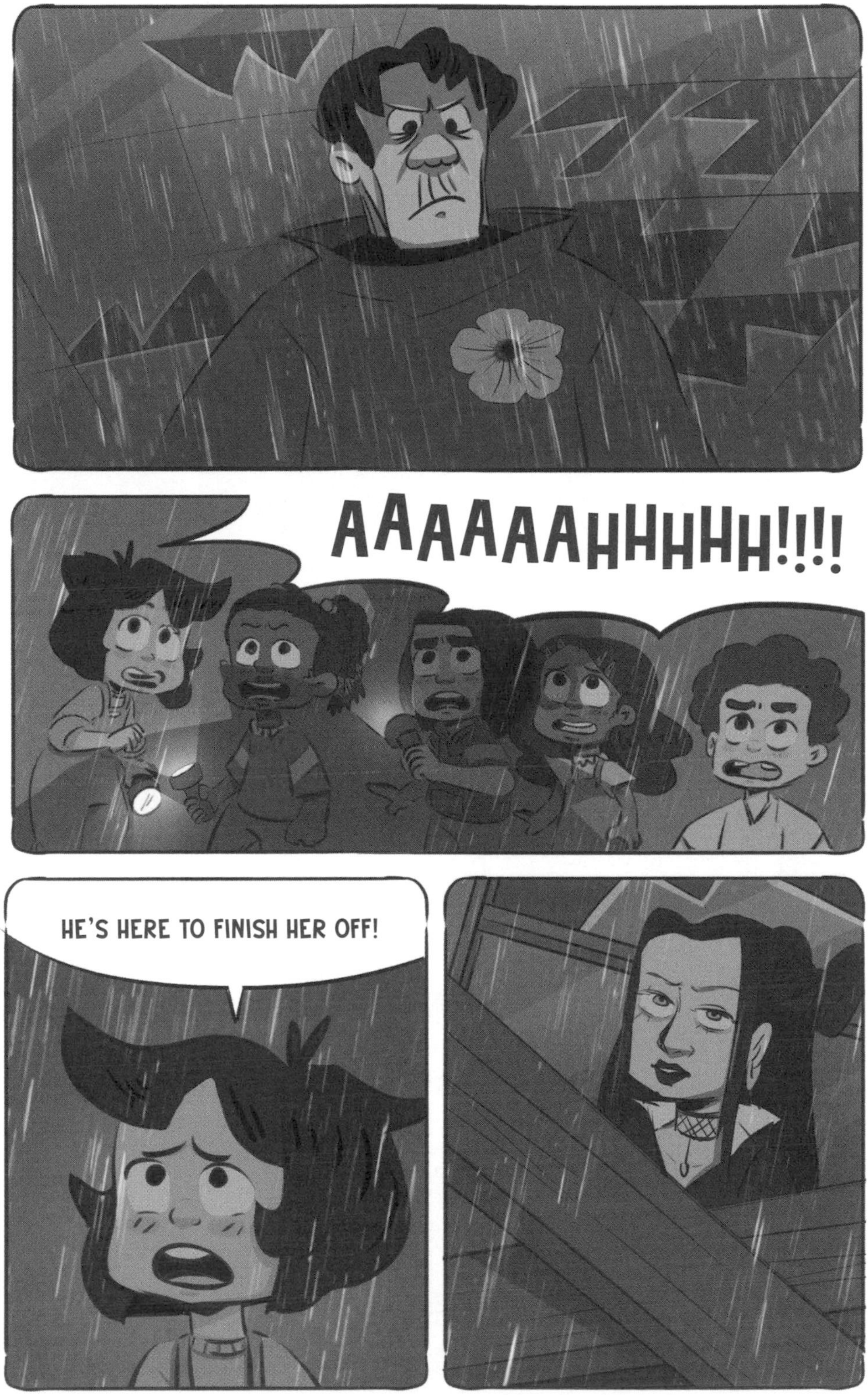
AAAAAAHHHHH!!!!
HE'S HERE TO FINISH HER OFF!

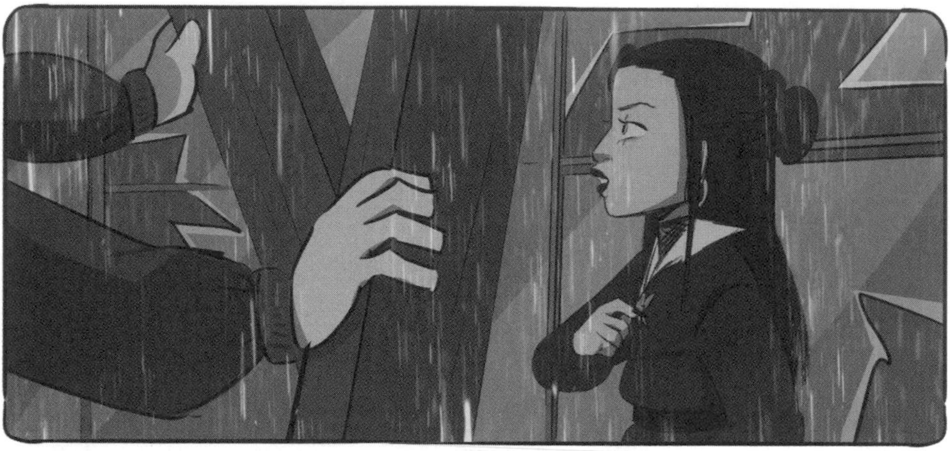

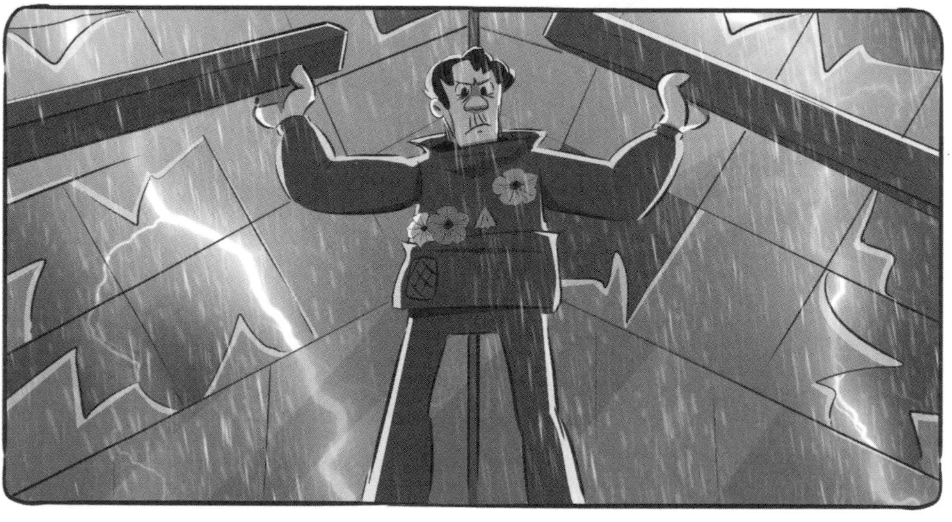

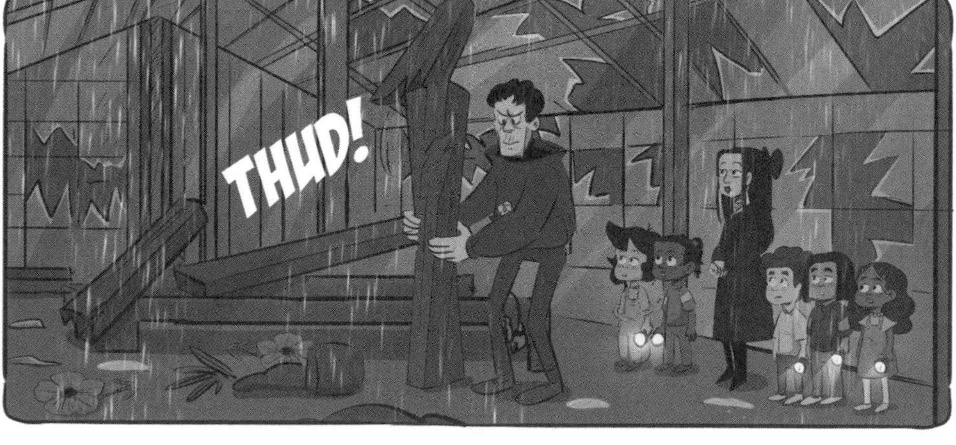
THUD!

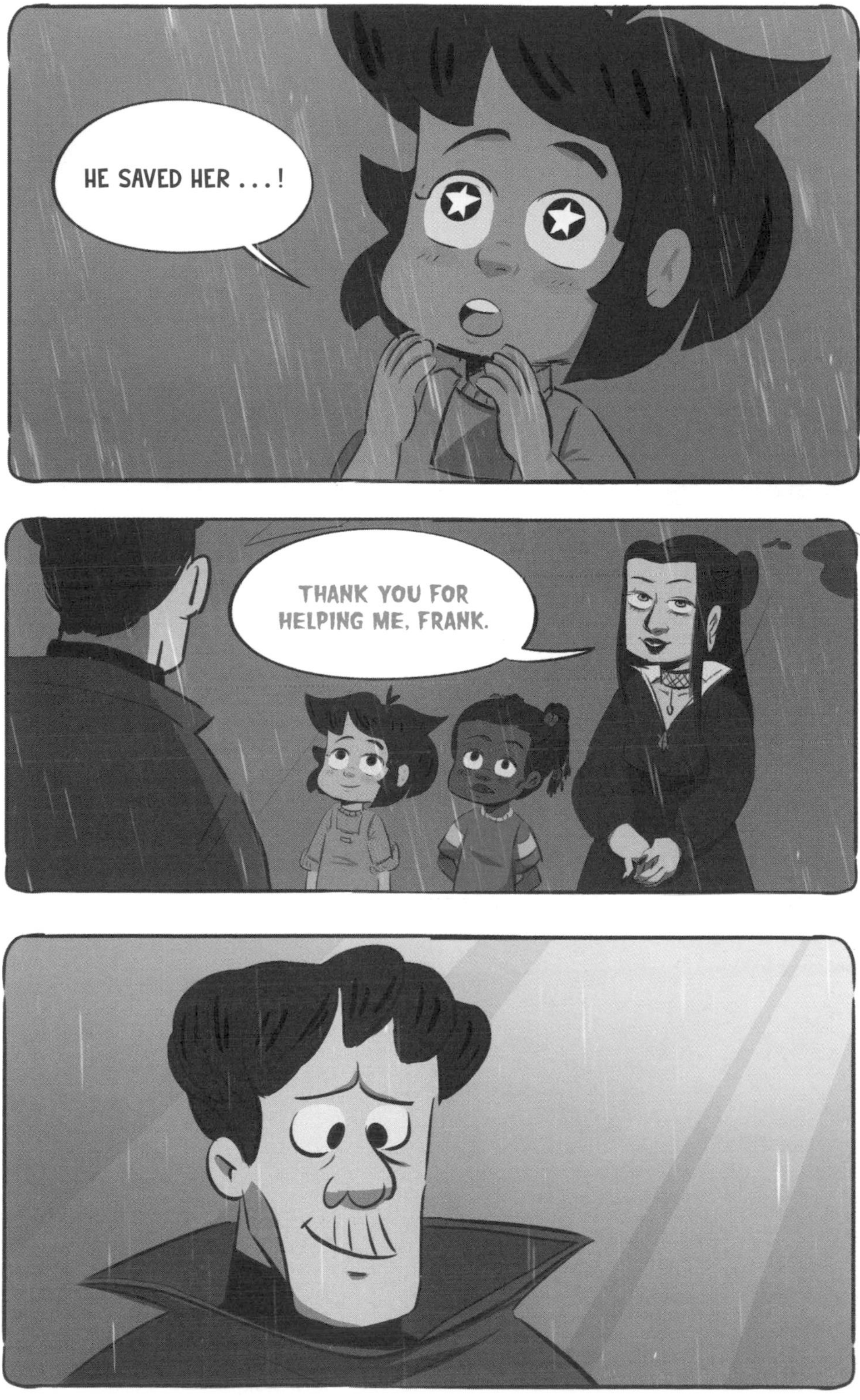
HE SAVED HER . . . !
THANK YOU FOR HELPING ME, FRANK.

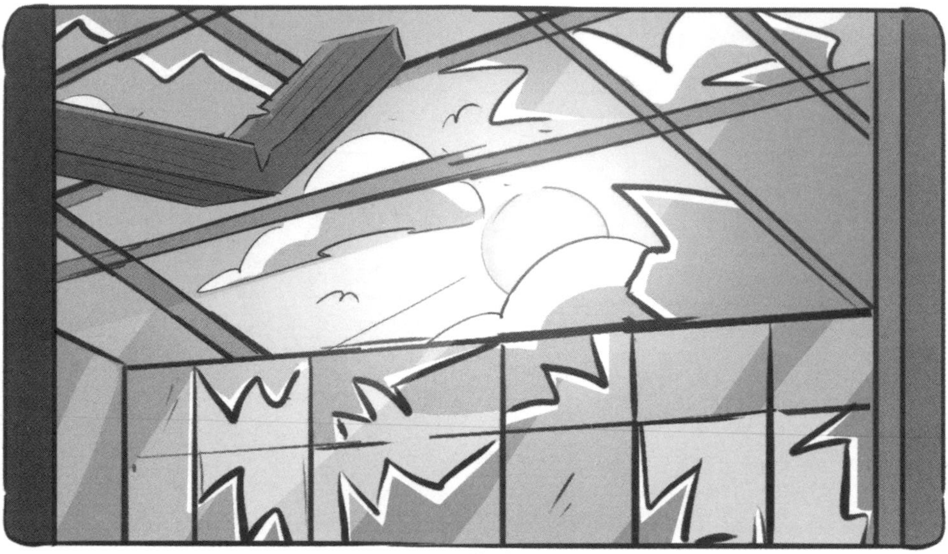

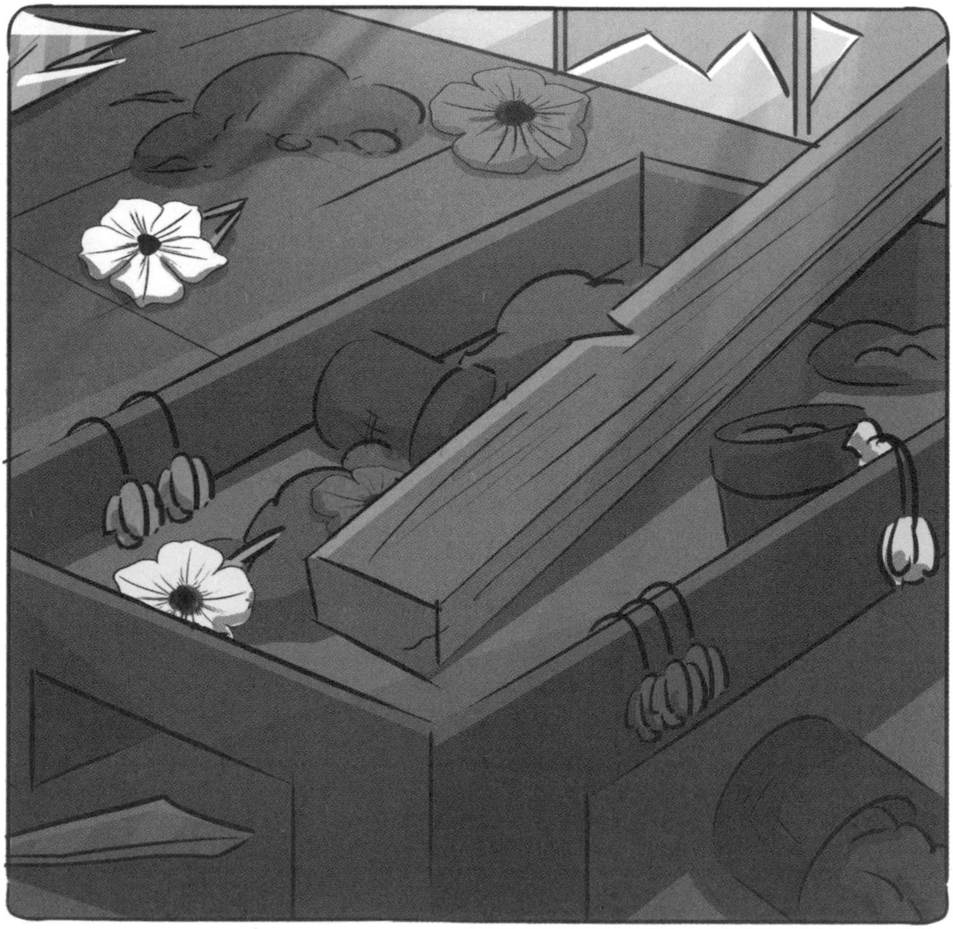

CHAPTER 5 PETUNIAS

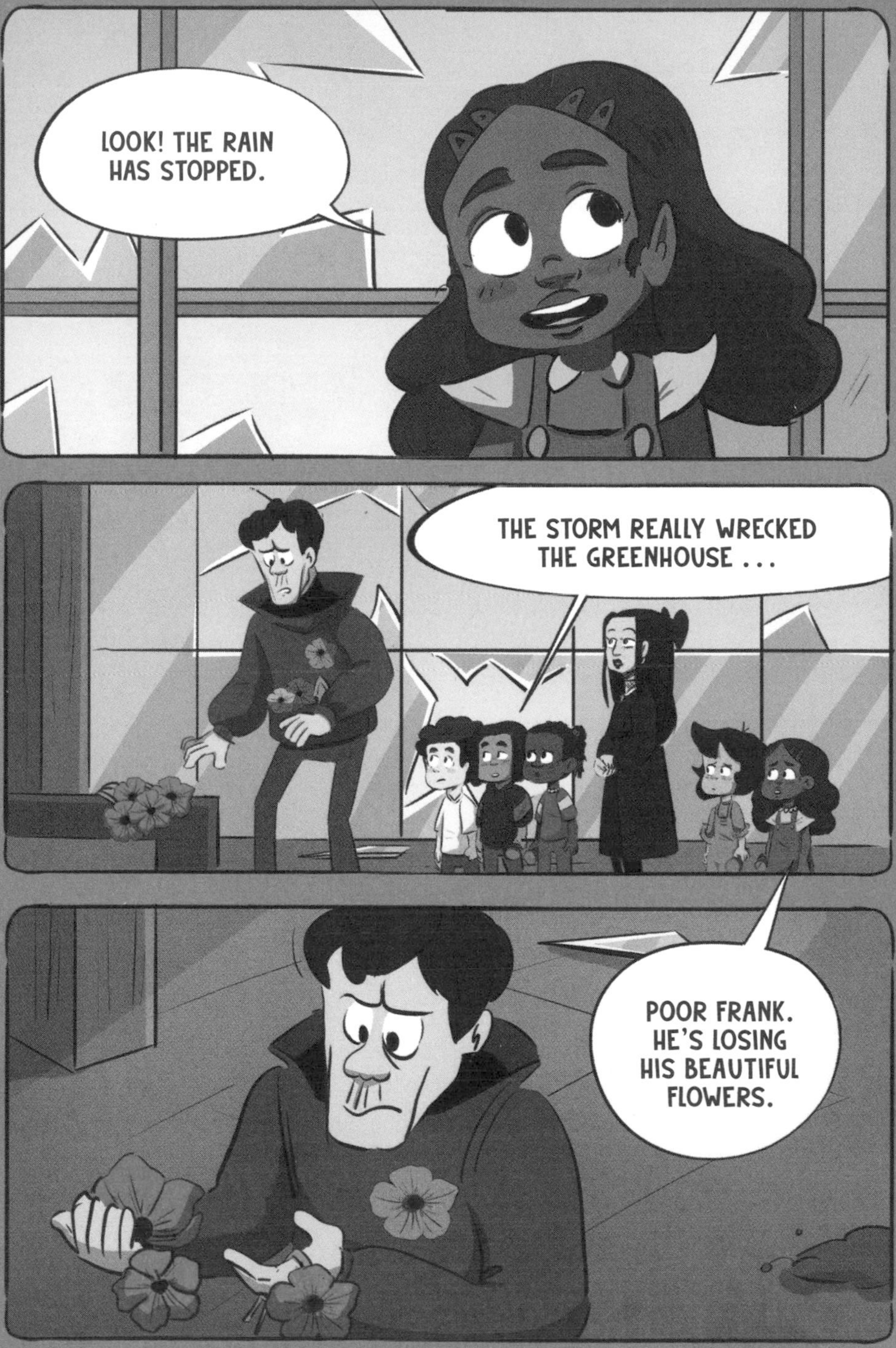
LOOK! THE RAIN HAS STOPPED.
THE STORM REALLY WRECKED THE GREENHOUSE . . .
POOR FRANK. HE'S LOSING HIS BEAUTIFUL FLOWERS.

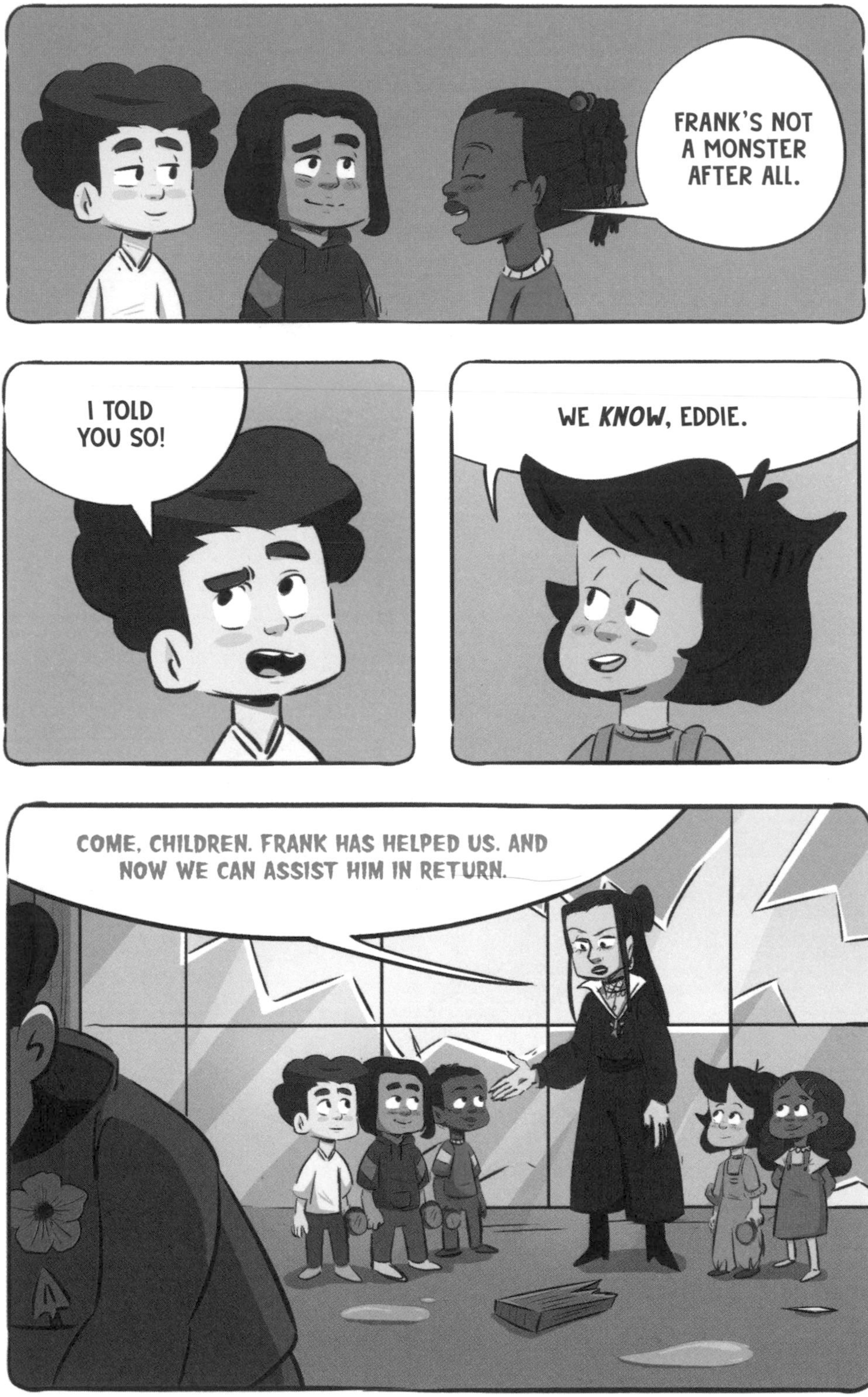
FRANK'S NOT A MONSTER AFTER ALL.
I TOLD YOU SO!
WE *KNOW*, EDDIE.
COME, CHILDREN. FRANK HAS HELPED US. AND NOW WE CAN ASSIST HIM IN RETURN.

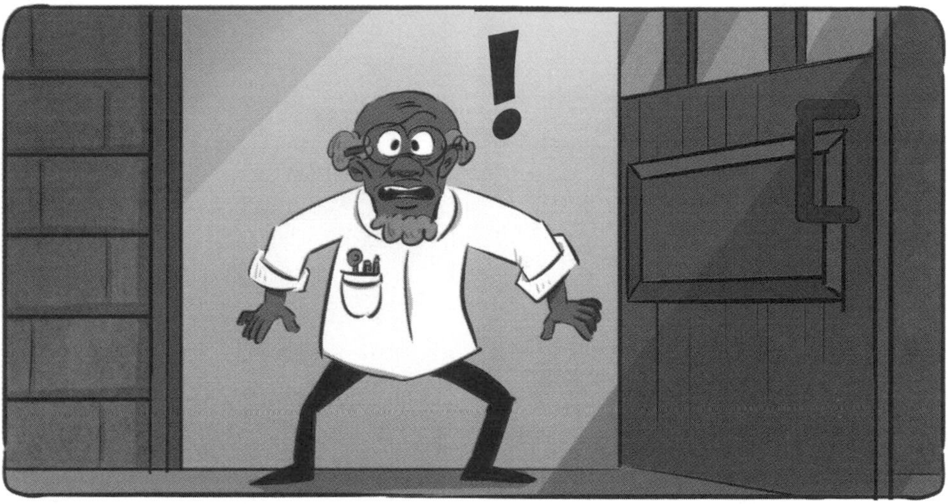
!

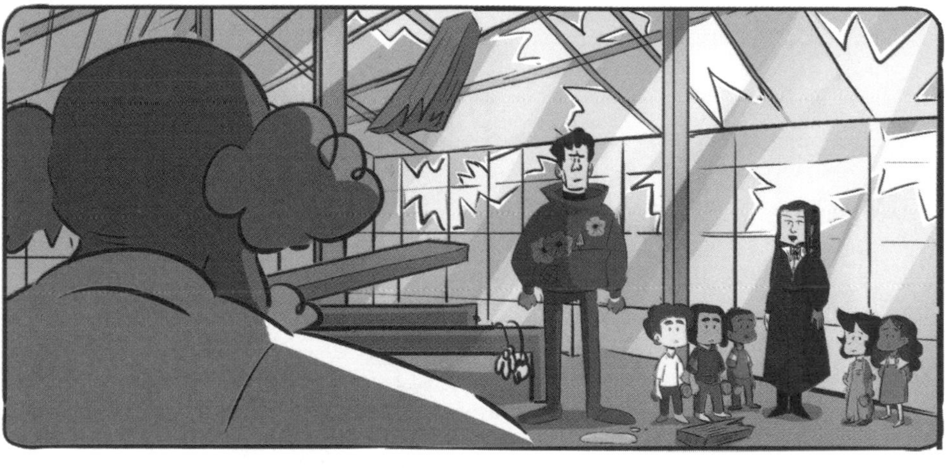

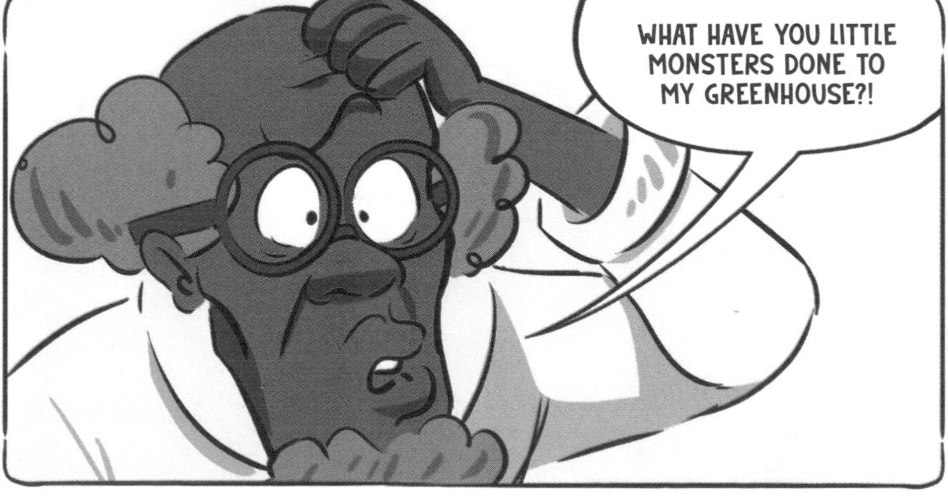
WHAT HAVE YOU LITTLE MONSTERS DONE TO MY GREENHOUSE?!

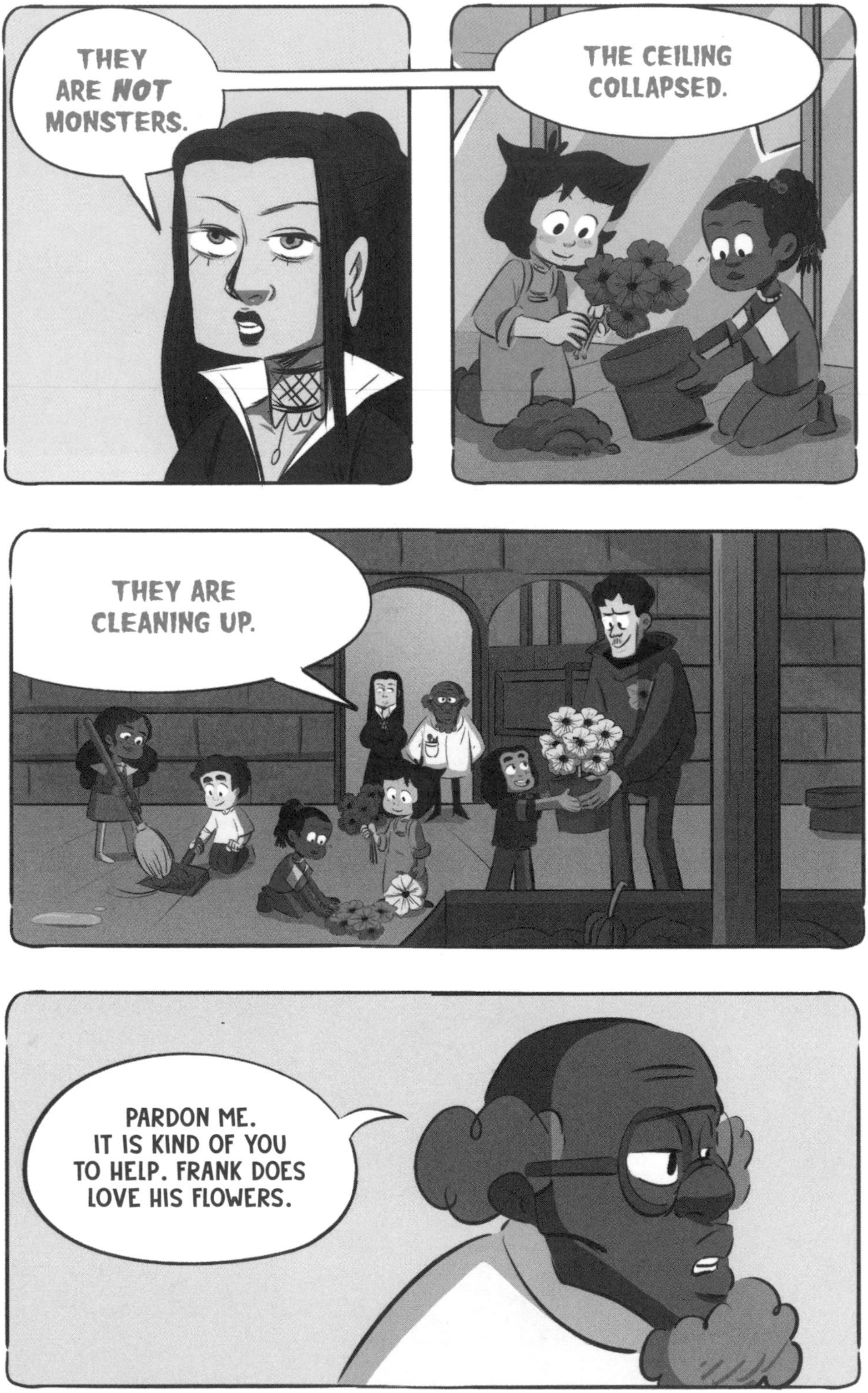
THEY ARE NOT MONSTERS.
THE CEILING COLLAPSED.
THEY ARE CLEANING UP.
PARDON ME. IT IS KIND OF YOU TO HELP. FRANK DOES LOVE HIS FLOWERS.

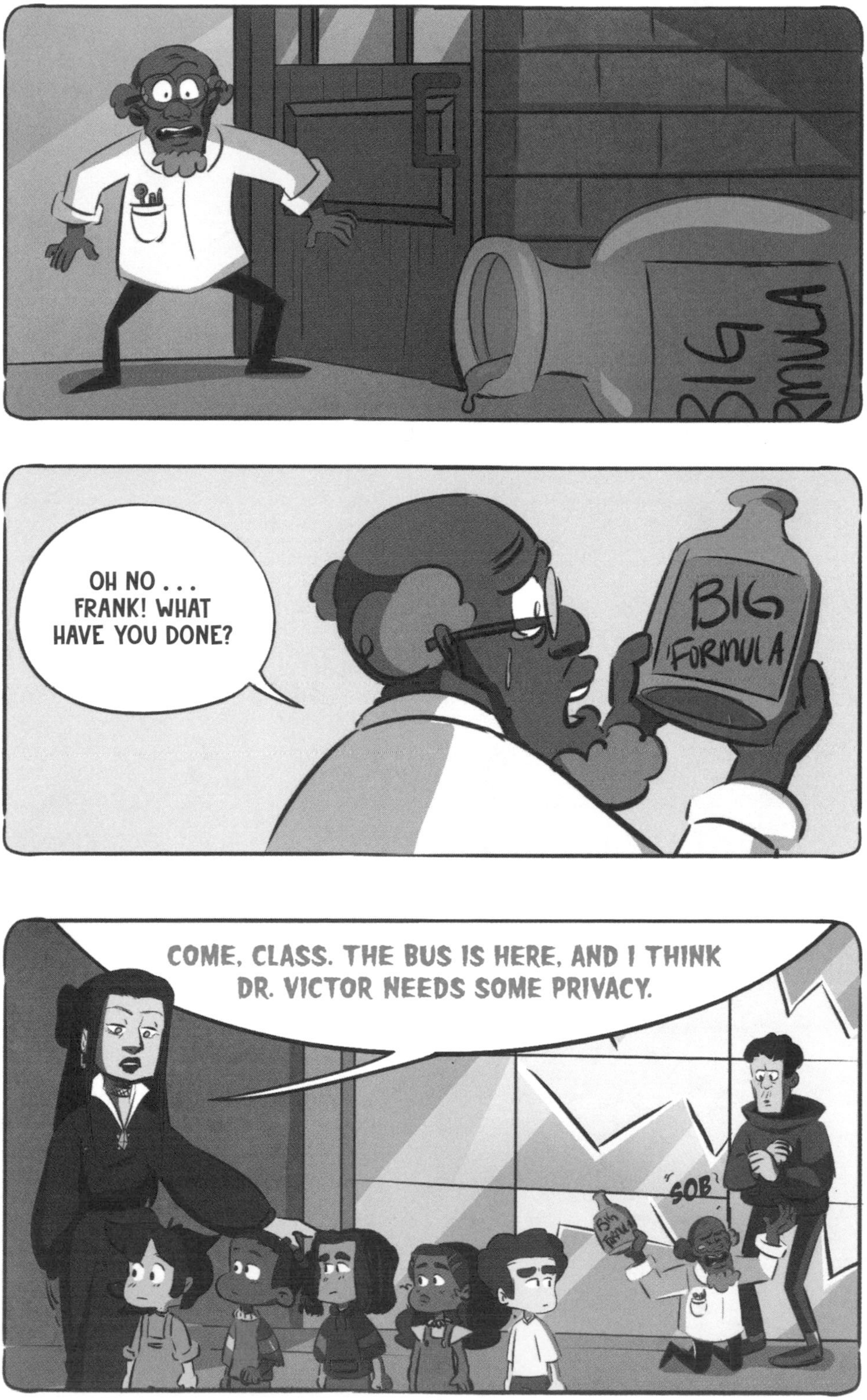
OH NO . . . FRANK! WHAT HAVE YOU DONE?
BIG FORMULA
COME, CLASS. THE BUS IS HERE, AND I THINK DR. VICTOR NEEDS SOME PRIVACY.
SOB

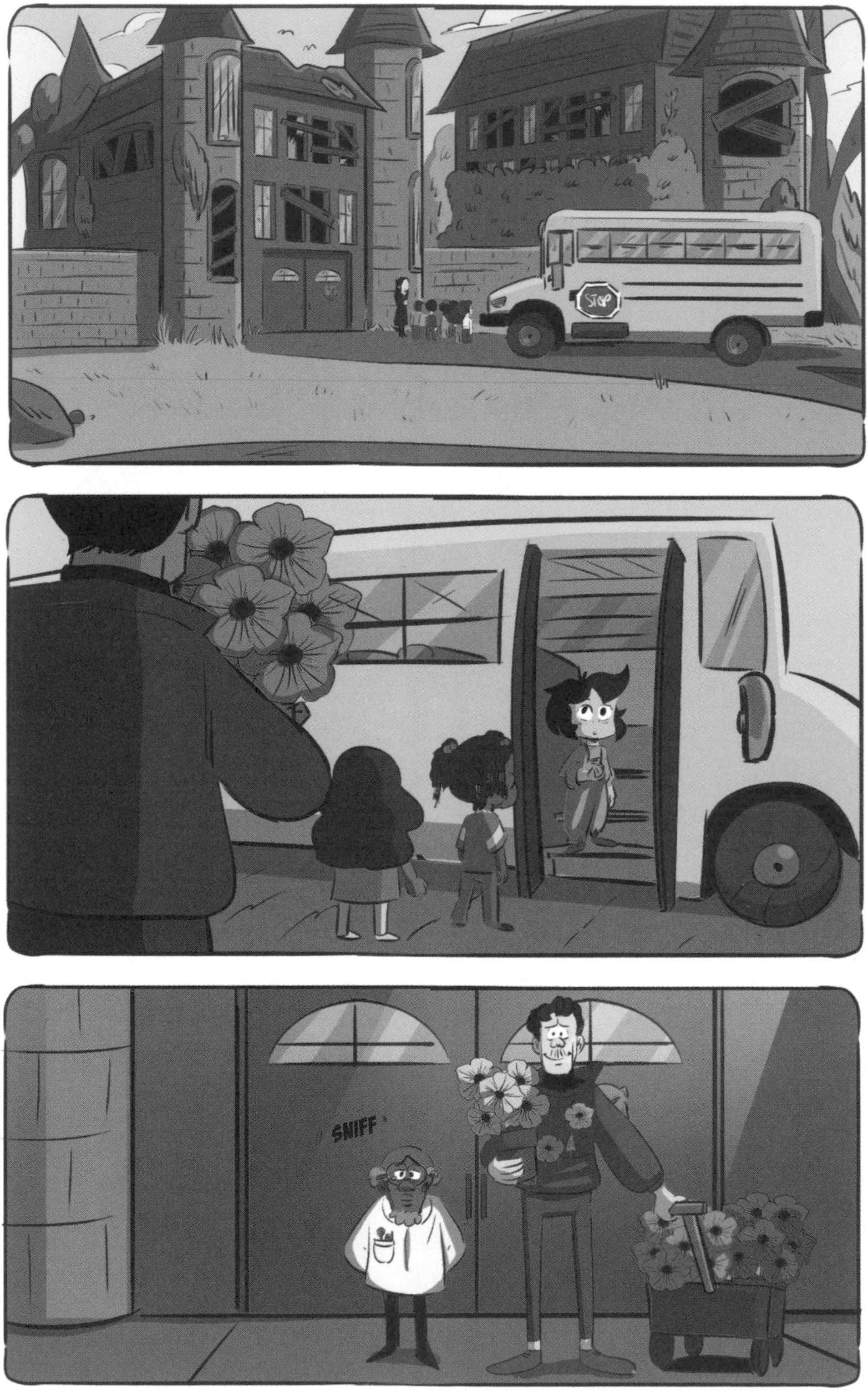
STOP
SNIFF

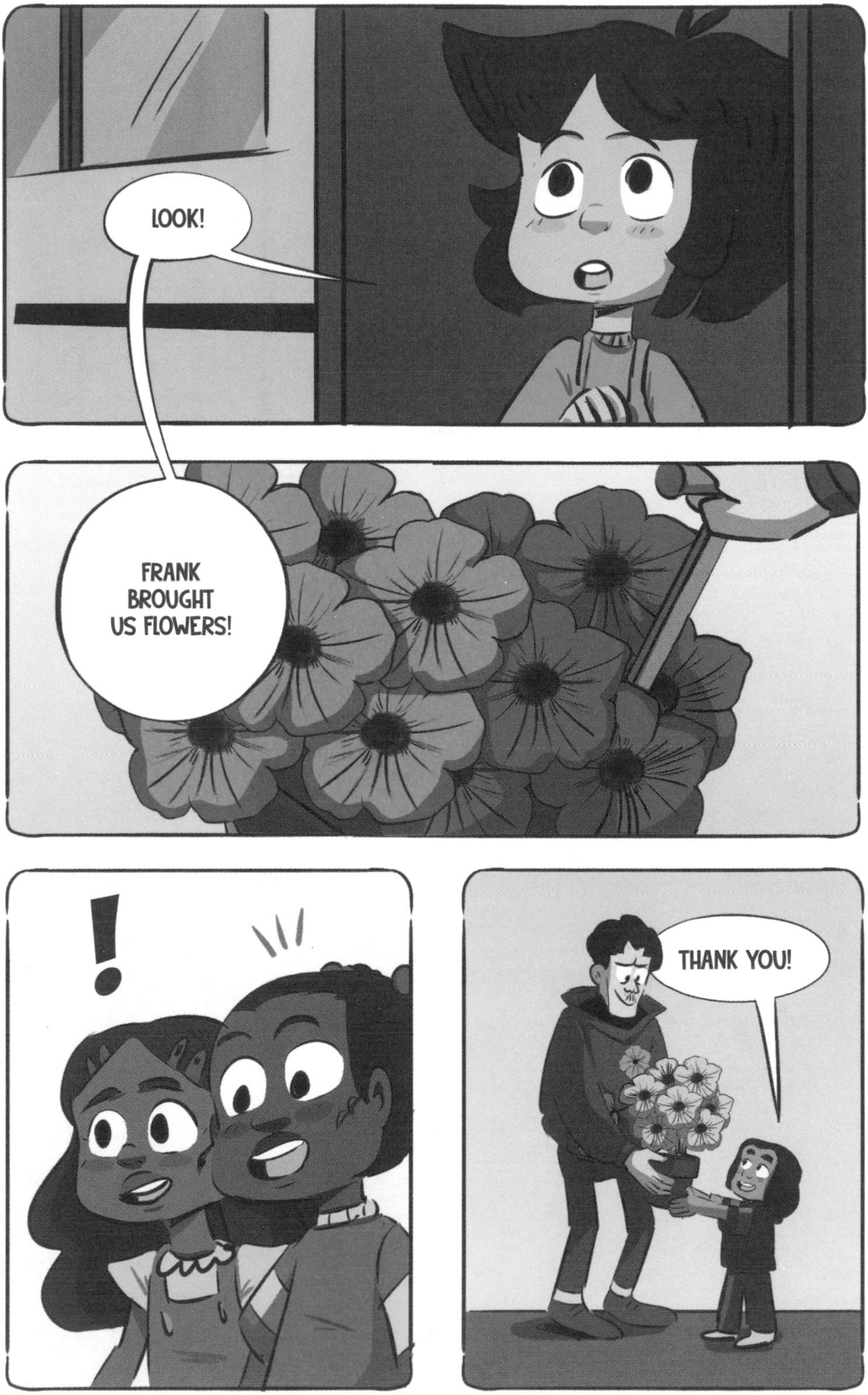
LOOK!
FRANK BROUGHT US FLOWERS!
!
THANK YOU!

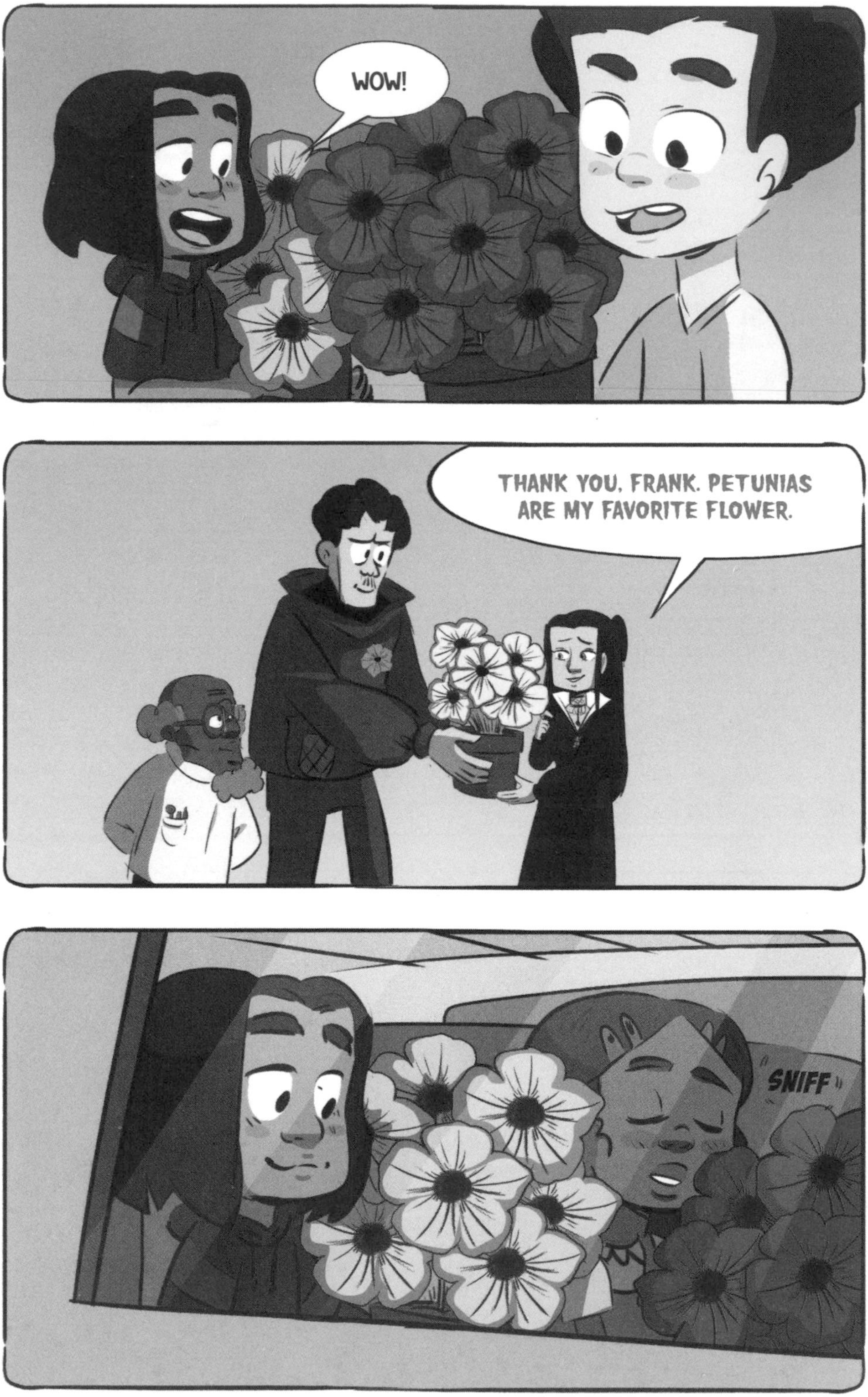
WOW!
THANK YOU, FRANK. PETUNIAS ARE MY FAVORITE FLOWER.
SNIFF

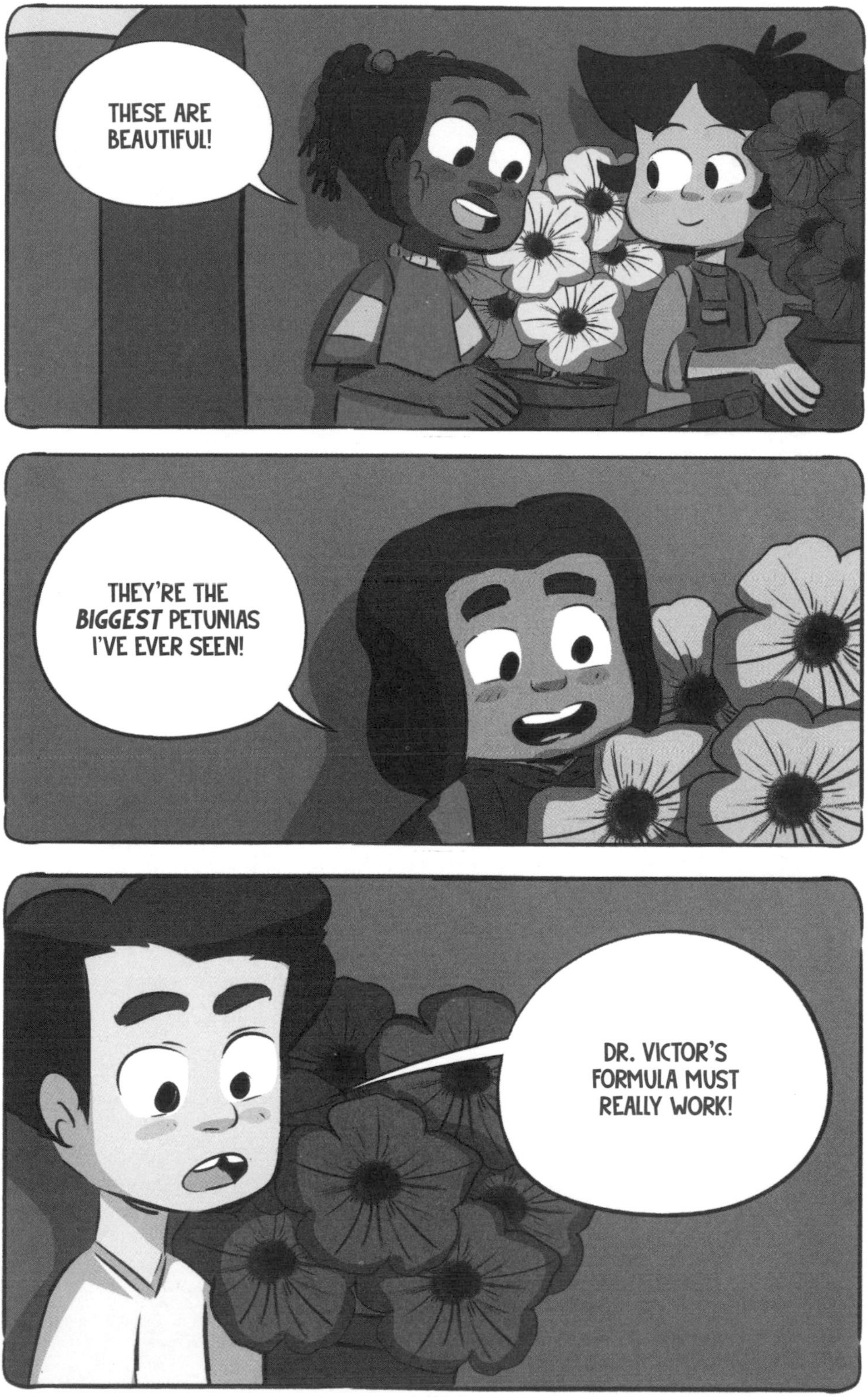
THESE ARE BEAUTIFUL!
THEY'RE THE *BIGGEST* PETUNIAS I'VE EVER SEEN!
DR. VICTOR'S FORMULA MUST REALLY WORK!

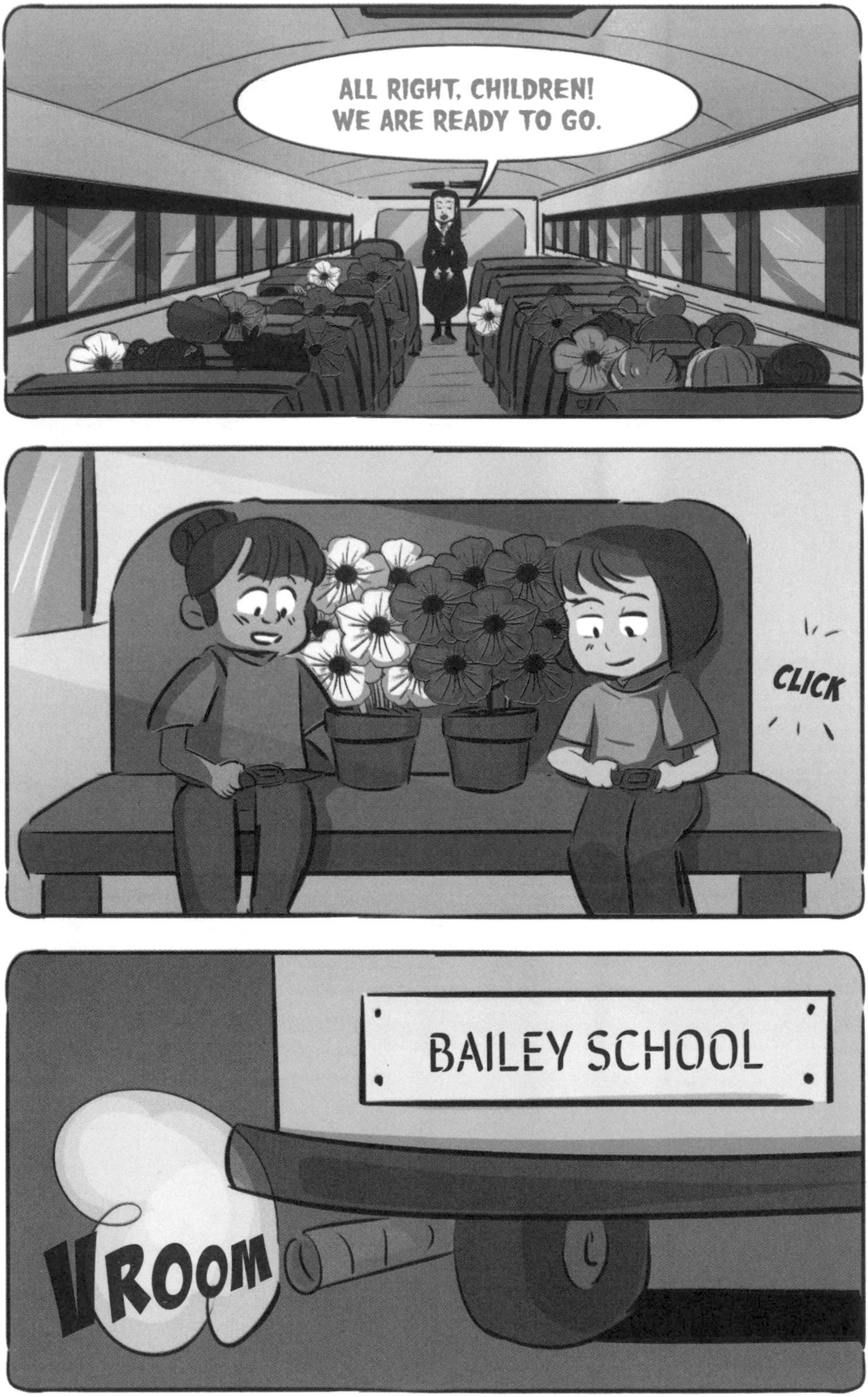
ALL RIGHT, CHILDREN! WE ARE READY TO GO.
CLICK
BAILEY SCHOOL
VROOM

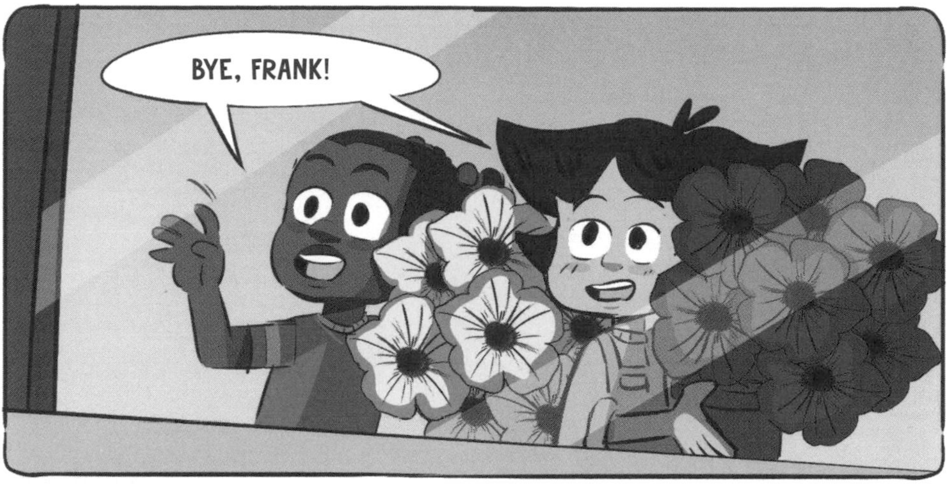
BYE, FRANK!

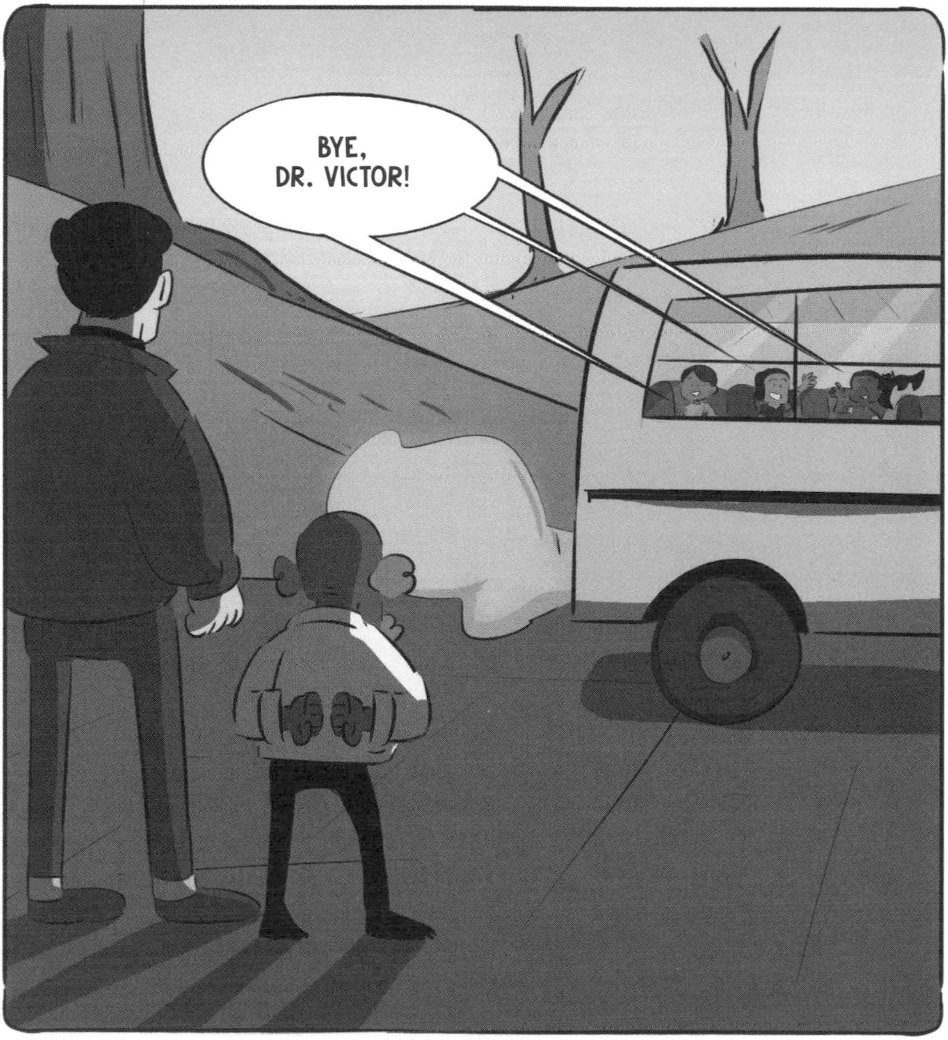
BYE,
DR. VICTOR!

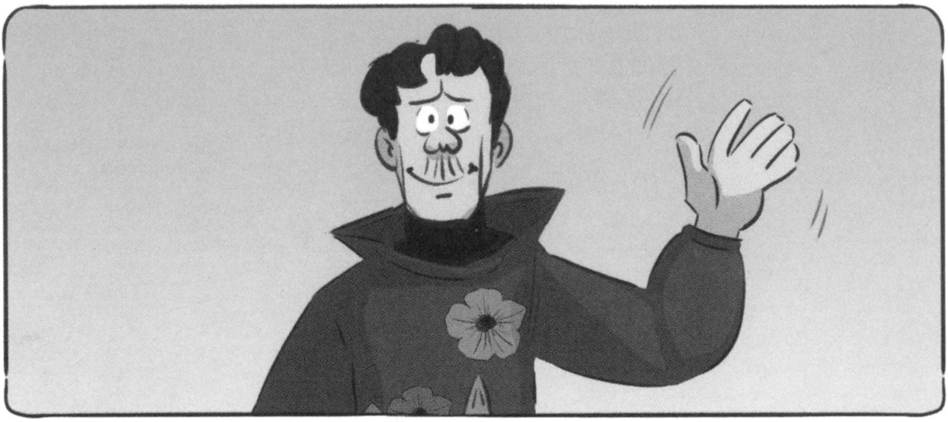

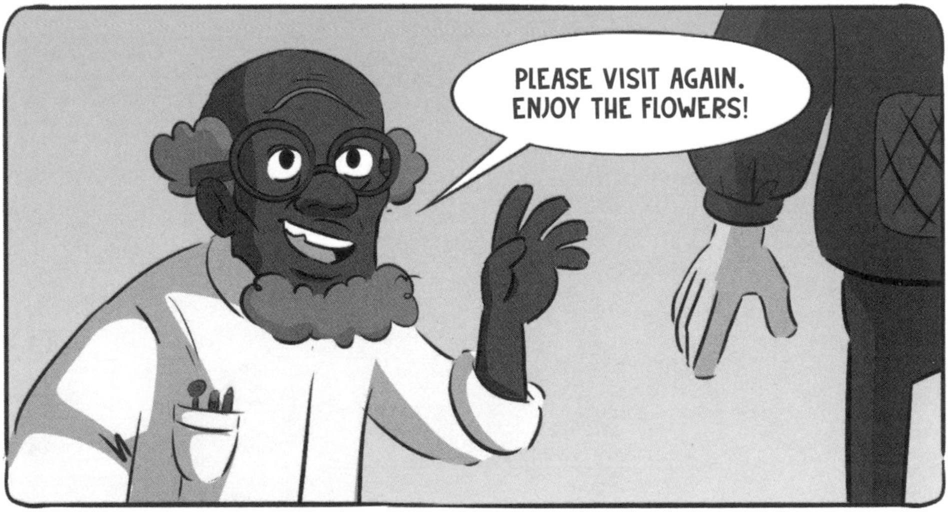
PLEASE VISIT AGAIN. ENJOY THE FLOWERS!

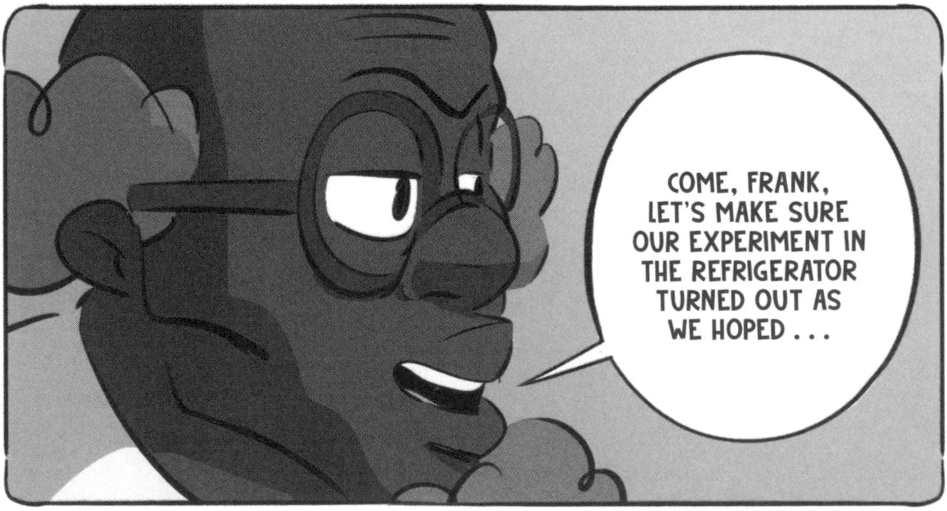
COME, FRANK, LET'S MAKE SURE OUR EXPERIMENT IN THE REFRIGERATOR TURNED OUT AS WE HOPED . . .

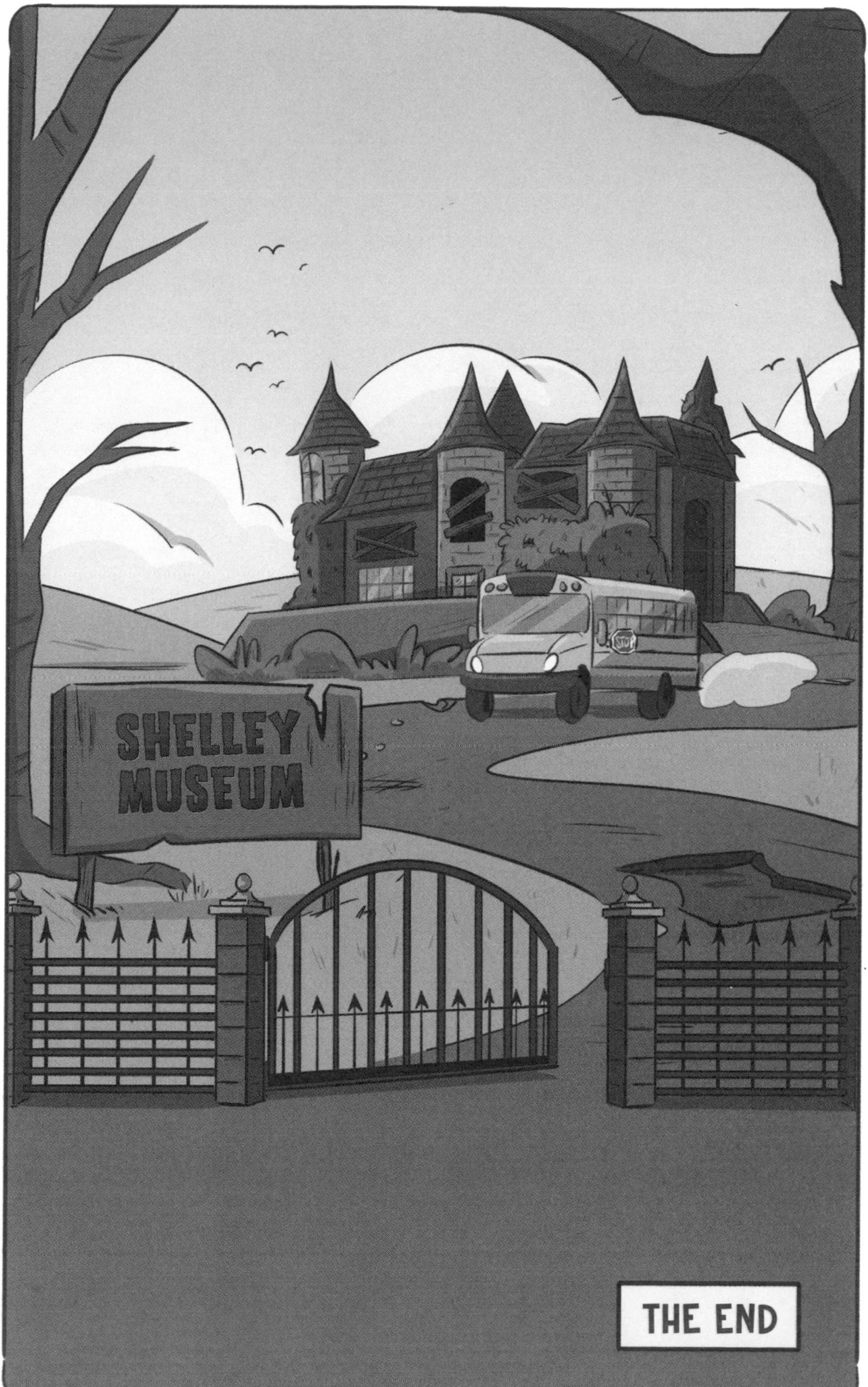
SHELLEY
MUSEUM
STOP
THE END

MARCIA THORNTON JONES is an award-winning author who has published more than 130 books for children, including the Adventures of the Bailey School Kids series, *Woodford Brave*, *Ratfink*, and *Champ*. Marcia lives with her husband, Steve, and two cats in Lexington, Kentucky, where she continues to write, mentor writers, and teach writing classes. She is the coordinator of the Carnegie Center Author Academy, an intensive one-on-one writing program for adult writers working toward publication.

DEBBIE DADEY grew up in Kentucky and now lives in a log cabin in Tennessee with her husband and two greyhound rescues. Her three adult children continue to inspire her. A former first grade teacher and school librarian, she is the author and coauthor of 180 books, including the Adventures of the Bailey School Kids series. Her newest series, Mermaid Tales, is a multicultural series from Simon and Schuster. She also coauthored *Writing for Kids: The Ultimate Guide* with Marcia Thornton Jones.

PEARL LOW is an Afro Asian artist based in Vancouver, Canada. Their art is rooted in themes of self-love, acceptance, and Chinese and Jamaican Canadian experiences. They work in comics and animation and won an Oscar in 2020 for their work on the short film *Hair Love*.